MXAC
9/2021

A King Production presents…

NO ONE MAN SHOULD HAVE ALL THAT POWER…BUT THERE WERE TWO

JOY DEJA KING

D1069334

This novel is a work of fiction. Any references to real people, events, establishments, or locales are intended only to give the fiction a sense of reality and authenticity. Other names, characters, and incidents occurring in the work are either the product of the author's imagination or are used fictitiously, as those fictionalized events and incidents that involve real persons. Any character that happens to share the name of a person who is an acquaintance of the author, past or present, is purely coincidental and is in no way intended to be an actual account involving that person.

ISBN 13: 978-1942217305
ISBN 10: 1-942217-30-7
Cover concept by Joy Deja King
Cover layout and graphic design by www.MarionDesigns.com

Library of Congress Cataloging-in-Publication Data;
A King Production
Power Part 2/by Joy Deja King
For complete Library of Congress Copyright info visit;
www.joydejaking.com
Twitter @joydejaking

A King Production
P.O. Box 912, Collierville, TN 38027

A King Production and the above portrayal log are trademarks of A King Production LLC

Copyright © 2019 by A King Production LLC. All rights reserved. No part of this book may be reproduced in any form without the permission from the publisher, except by reviewer who may quote brief passage to be printed in a newspaper or magazine.

This Book is Dedicated To My:

Family, Readers, and Supporters.
I LOVE you guys so much. Please believe that!!

—Joy Deja King

"There's one life, one love, so there can only be one king…"

—Nas

Chapter 1
PROMISES

Alex stood on the balcony of his penthouse apartment watching as the sun came up. The peaceful Atlanta skyline masked the furor that was burning inside Alex's heart. He hadn't slept at all. After that cryptic phone call he received last night, his mind went into overdrive. He held on tightly to his cell, waiting for the person to call back. Realistically he knew it wouldn't happen this early in the morning, but his hunger for the truth outweighed logic.

"What the fuck is really going on," Alex barked loudly, pushing open the glass French doors that led back into his bedroom. "Is somebody playing some type of sick game with me or was the Get Money

Crew really not behind Dahlia's death?" he asked himself out loud as if miraculously the question would be answered for him.

Alex walked over to the dresser and reached for the picture frame of Dahlia. She was smiling and her face radiated beauty. Little did either of them know that less than a week after the photo was taken, Dahlia would be dead. Tears swelled up in Alex's eyes, but they didn't fall, he wouldn't allow them to. Instead, he let his anger take over.

"I will spend the rest of my life murdering anyone that had something to do with your death. I promise you, baby," Alex said, placing his hand on Dahlia's face before putting the picture down.

Deion let the hot water drench over his body in the shower as if trying to baptize away all the sin he had committed. For a moment he thought he saw blood going down the drain and had to close then reopen his eyes to make sure his mind wasn't playing tricks on him. But there was no blood, only clear water that represented the purity Deion lacked.

Reminiscing over the blood bath the he, Alex, and their crew committed on GMC, momentarily made Deion forget about the call he received from Demonte last night. But once he stepped out of the shower and saw the missed calls from Passion, he quickly remembered. Before he could even call back, his phone began ringing again.

"Yo," Deion answered coolly.

"Nigga, you must want me to put a bullet in yo' ho and her son since you don't know how to answer yo' fuckin' phone."

"Chill, I was in the shower."

"You betta keep yo' phone on you even when you shittin' nigga, if you know what's good for you. 'Cause next time I can't get ahold of you, I'm sending body parts through the mail."

Deion held the phone away from his ear and looked at it for a second. He couldn't believe the dude on the other end was poppin' so much shit. He was about to tell him to go fuck himself and hang up, but an image of Demonte flashed in his head, so he decided to bite his tongue.

"Hello! You there motherfucker?"

"Yeah, I'm here. So what that price looking like?" Deion asked, wanting to get right down to it because the longer he stayed on the phone with the dude, the angrier he was becoming.

"I need two hundred and fifty."

"Two hundred and fifty what?" Deion shot back like he knew the dude couldn't possibly be asking what he thought he was asking for.

"What you think, nigga? Two hundred and fifty thousand. If I don't get it, this broad and her child is dead. Now what's it gon' be?"

"It's yours."

"I'll call you back in a couple hours to let you know where to drop it off at and you betta have my money together by then."

"It's your world my nigga. Whatever you want." Deion hung up knowing that whoever the motherfucker was on the other end of the phone, he would never get a dime out of him. That was a promise and he put that on his life.

Chapter 2
FOLLOW YOUR INSTINCTS

"I'ma need to gather up some of the crew and them niggas gotta be strapped and ready," Deion said, the moment he walked into the lounge Reggie recently opened in the Atlantic Station area.

"Damn, we just had them light up GMC at Fire and Ice, you want to put them back to work already?"

"Yeah, I ain't got no choice," Deion said, taking a seat at the bar.

"What bullshit you done got involved wit' now?"

"Man, remember when I told you about that explosion at Passion's crib?"

"Yeah, you said it killed her and her lil' man."

"Well, they alive and some motherfucker using them as a ransom, tryna get two hundred and fifty thousand outta me."

"Word? And you gon' pay it?" Reggie asked.

"Hell no!"

"You gon' let them die?"

"Nah, I can't let Demonte die. He a good kid."

"You got a lot of fucked up ways but you do love the kids."

"No doubt that's why I gotta get this crew together, 'cause I ain't gon' let Demonte die. I'm also not about to give that nigga not a dolla of my paper. That," Deion said, putting his finger up, "ain't gonna happen."

"So what's the plan? Do you know who got them held up?"

"Nope, but I gotta feeling it's the same dude that killed Popcorn."

"So how we gon' get..." Reggie stopped mid-sentence. Both men turned towards the entrance as Alex walked through the door.

"Did I interrupt something? You both staring at me like I caught you in the middle of plotting some shit."

"Actually you did," Deion admitted. "Passion and her son didn't get killed in that explosion I told you about. Some nigga kidnapped them and now want a ransom to be paid for their release. I got the call last night."

"Damn, I guess we both didn't sleep last night."

"And here I thought you would've slept like a baby now that you got retribution for Dahlia," Deion stated, lighting up a Newport.

"Maybe I didn't get retribution."

"Huh?" Reggie frowned. "We just demolished an entire crew. Ain't nobody left. So what's left to do?" he questioned.

"I thought we was done with it too, until..."

"Until what?" Deion interrupted.

"Until I got a call last night saying that if I wanted to know who killed my fiancé then to meet them."

"What the fuck! Man, that's probably somebody playing a sick fuckin' joke on you," Reggie rationalized, shaking his head.

"You might be right or the shit could be legit

but I won't be able to rest until I know for sure. Everyone responsible for Dahlia's murder will be held accountable."

"I dig that man," Reggie said, as he stocked the bar. "You look like you need a drink. Can I get you something?"

"No, I'm straight."

"So when are you supposed to get this info?" Deion questioned nonchalantly, trying to appear as if he wasn't pressed.

"She said she would call back today. I've been holding my cell so motherfuckin' close to the palm of my hand the shit feeling glued on."

As Reggie and Alex went back and forth discussing who could've reached out to him and if it was legit, Deion was digging deep in his brain wondering who the fuck could've called Alex. Deion thought for sure his secret had died with Tommy but now he wasn't sure. *Could somebody just be fuckin' with Alex or was there really somebody else out there that knows the truth? I can't take those types of chances,* Deion thought as he continued searching his mind for answers.

"Why you so quiet?" Reggie asked, breaking Deion out of his thoughts. "You always got some shit to say."

"I got a lot on my mind. You know, thinkin' 'bout Passion and Demonte," Deion said putting his cigarette out in the ashtray.

"Have you figured out how you want to handle it?" Alex questioned.

"Yeah, I'm 'bout to round some of our men up so we handle the nigga when he come get the money."

"Watch yo'self, man. You don't know what type of motherfucker you dealing with," Alex warned. "You want me to come with you?" he offered.

"Nah, I'm good. Plus, you need to wait on that phone call. But I need to go. Just got the text from Bernard letting me know the men are at the warehouse. I'll hit you later on and let you know what happens."

"Cool."

"We here if you need us," Reggie added before Deion walked out. "I hope Deion know what he doing," Reggie commented after the door shut.

"He'll figure it out and if he doesn't, trust me, he'll call."

"Since we back on the subject of calls, what you gon' do 'bout the one you got?"

"Just wait, I guess."

"If I was you, I wouldn't get my hopes up."

"Why?"

"'Cause I think we got the right niggas. Remember you found the GMC baggie of drugs there. I'm tellin' you it was them. Them niggas stepped to you on some foul shit, tryna be sweet. They just never expected you to come back at them so hard. That's what them motherfuckers get."

"Maybe you right," Alex said, resting his hand over his mouth, as he leaned on the bar. "But why would somebody call my phone in the middle of the night and say some shit like that?" Alex wondered out loud, shaking his head.

"Man, listen. There are some heartless fucks out here. Some simple broad wit' too much time on her hands probably playin' on the phone."

"I think I do need that drink," Alex stated, taking a seat. Alex's head was agreeing with Reggie but his gut was telling him something else. Under normal circumstances Alex would always follow his gut instincts but he knew Dahlia's murder had him emotional. He tried to never make decisions based on those types of feelings and it had worked in his favor thus far. Alex held his phone tightly, staring at it; *maybe it was the Get Money Crew after all,* he thought before slamming his phone down on the bar.

Chapter 3
TAKE IT IN BLOOD

"This nigga still ain't hit me back yet," Deion said, glancing down at his watch. "Bernard, you stay here with the rest of the men. I have to take care of something. When it's time to move, I'll hit you up."

"We ready, boss. Just give me the word."

Deion nodded his head at Bernard and walked out the warehouse heading to his car. Although he was ready to get this situation with Passion dealt with, Deion was actually pleased that the kidnapper hadn't called yet. It gave him the extra time he needed to follow a hunch.

Deion drove to an apartment complex in the College Park area. He parked his silver G63 AMG in the back parking lot. Before making his exit, he flipped through his contacts until coming to the number he was looking for. He dialed the number and when the person picked up after the third ring, Deion made his move. As he headed towards the apartment, he looked around making sure nobody was watching him. He knocked on the door located on the second floor. Deion waited for a few seconds then knocked again. He knew someone was there because they had just answered the landline less than a minute ago. Right when Deion was about to knock again he could hear someone coming. Deion stepped to the side so they couldn't see him.

"Who is it?"

"Building maintenance. The tenants below you complained about a leak. It's coming from your apartment."

"I don't know where the leak can be coming from, but you can..." before the door was even completely open, Deion had reached in the back of his jeans, pulling out his Glock .40 and pushed his way in. "Please don't hurt me!" the woman screamed.

"Shut the fuck up!" Deion barked, shoving

the tip of his gun in the girl's open mouth. Her jaw began pulsating like she wanted to vomit. "When I take this gun out yo' mouth, you bet not scream."

She nodded her head yes while the tears flowed. Deion slammed the door shut, locking it and latching the chain. "I want you to sit down and don't speak until spoken to or I'ma knock you upside the head wit' this gun. You understand?" The scared woman nodded her head as her eyes widened in fear.

"Who are you? What do you want from me?" the woman asked between sniffles.

"Didn't I tell you not to speak until spoken to?" Deion snarled, raising his gun up like he was going to strike her with it.

"I'm sorry! I'm sorry! Please don't hit me!" the woman pleaded.

"Let's try this again. I'ma ask you some questions and I want you to tell me the truth. If you answer honestly, we might be able to come to an understanding."

"Okay."

"A woman called my partner Alex telling him

she had some information about his girlfriend's murder. At first I couldn't figure out who could've made that call, but then I remembered Tommy had a girl that lived wit' him. You know how niggas like to pillow talk. I'm willing to bet good money that's what happened wit' you. Ain't that right?"

"No, I don't know what you talkin' about," she said shaking her head.

"Where yo' cell phone at?"

"Huh?"

"Don't 'huh' me. Where's yo' fuckin' cell phone?"

"I don't have a cell phone."

"This ain't gon' end well for you," Deion said, grabbing the woman by her hair.

"I swear I don't have a phone. I stayed in the house most of the time so Tommy would just call the house number."

"For yo' sake you betta be tellin' the truth," Deion threatened, dragging the woman from room to room. After going through the three-bedroom apartment and not finding anything, Deion started thinking that as crazy as it sounded the woman might be telling the truth. But on the second go round he noticed a pink and yellow iPhone 5c on top of the bathroom sink. "What do we have here." Deion chuckled, reaching for the cell. He went to her recent calls and scanned down the numbers until coming across a *67 in front of Alex's digits. "You should've never lied to me. I told you it wouldn't end well."

"Let me explain... I'm sorry," she cried. From that moment the woman got diarrhea of the mouth. "When I got word that everybody in GMC got killed including Tommy, I couldn't understand why. Then one of my homegirls told me that her man said that it was in retaliation for them killing this dude named Alex's girl. But I knew that had to be a lie because Tommy told me that a guy he was trying to do business with named Deion, killed her 'cause she was a snitch. A guy I'm cool with had Alex's phone number and he gave it to me. I just wanted him to know the truth. He killed an innocent man and they entire crew for nothing. The nigga he really needed to get was Deion."

"Who else did you tell?"

"Nobody."

"Don't lie to me," Deion said, tightening his grip on her.

"I'm not."

"What's yo' name?"

"Tania," she answered with a trembly voice.

"Tania, I don't believe you. I think you got a big mouth just like yo' dead boyfriend Tommy."

"No, I swear. I was waiting for my homegirl to call me to make sure it was really Alex and his people that did the shooting. I didn't wanna start no mess until I knew for sure. Look at my phone. I only called the dude Alex once."

"You called him one too many times, Tania."

"What you mean... why you say that?" she said confused.

"Don't you get it, you dumb broad. I'm Deion."

"Wait... wait... wait.... I won't say nothing. I promise."

"I know you won't," Deion said, grabbing a throw pillow off the couch and placing it over her face before busting three shots to her head. Tania's dead body slumped to the floor and that's exactly where Deion left it before walking out.

Chapter 4
THE SET UP

"Alex, it's so good to hear from you." Isabella smiled, as she lounged by the pool at the W South Beach.

"It's good to hear your voice, too. Listen, I need to meet with you."

"Business or pleasure?" she asked, sipping on her Bellini.

"Business."

"I'm disappointed, Alex. But I can put my feelings aside."

"Good, because I want back in. Are you in town?"

"No, I'm in Miami right now. I'll be here for the next few days. I can be to you by the weekend."

"That works."

"I look forward to seeing you, Alex."

"Enjoy your trip, Isabella. I'll see you soon."

After Alex ended his call with Isabella he sat down on the couch and stared up at the vaulted ceiling, deep in thought. Less than a week ago, Alex was done with the game. He was planning his future with Dahlia, their baby, and making his money legitimately. Those dreams died with his fiancé. Although Alex didn't need the money, he now needed the thrill of hustling to get him through his grief. If he didn't have something to occupy his time, he knew he would be consumed with thoughts of Dahlia and it would drive him crazy. Alex figured if he couldn't spend the rest of his life with the woman he loved then he might as well stay married to the streets.

"You still ain't heard nothin'?" Bernard asked when Deion arrived back at the warehouse.

"Nope. I don't know what the fuck is going

on. Clearly somebody playin' games and I don't like this shit at all," Deion responded, running his hands across the array of guns laid out on the table.

"So what you want us to do?"

"Maybe we need to shut it down for today. Ya been sittin' 'round here for hours. Here…" Deion said, reaching in his pocket taking out a wad of cash. "Pay the men for their time," he continued, handing the money to Bernard.

Not a second after dismissing the workers, Deion's phone started ringing. As if sensing this might be the call, Bernard stopped in his tracks and turned back towards Deion, who put his finger up, motioning for him to wait a sec. "Hello."

"Hope you got my money ready."

"I been had yo' money ready." Deion nodded his head at Bernard letting him know it was about to go down. "You the one that's…" Deion paused and looked down at his watch, "over six hours late."

"You on my time so don't worry about me being late."

"It's all good."

"I want you to drive to the Exxon on Monroe

Drive, NE. I'll hit you back shortly."

"Yo, I wanna speak to Passion and Demonte."

"Didn't I tell you, you on my time."

"Listen, if you don't put them on the phone so I know they straight, then we can forget this shit right now."

"Hold on," the man grumbled. There was a long silence before what sounded like an out of breath Passion got on the phone.

"Hello," Passion huffed.

"You and Demonte okay?"

"Yeah, but I'm scared, Deion," she said. It was obvious that Passion was now crying.

"He didn't do nothing to you, did he?" Deion asked with hesitation. Deion was well aware of the impact rape could have on a woman and although he had committed rape himself he would never want it to happen to Passion.

"No... no," she cried, "but..."

"That's enough talking," the man barked, grabbing the phone from Passion.

"Now put Demonte on the phone."

"Uncle Deion, are you going to bring us home?"

"Yes. Just take care of yo' mother. I'll see you both soon."

"A'right, you talked to them. Now bring me my motherfuckin' money."

"I'm headed to Exxon now," Deion said, ending the call. "It's time to play, fellas. Get ya guns ready. Time to move."

Clifton Jones aka Clip stood with his hands in his black slacks at the cemetery. Only minutes ago the place was filled with hundreds of people but now they were gone. He waited until everyone had left before getting out of his limo to pay his respects. He watched as the last casket went into the ground. That could've easily been him. Clip was the only member of the Get Money Crew not in attendance at Fire and Ice when the hit went down. Normally, he would've never missed the meeting, especially since he was second in command of the entire operation. But Clip was needed on the East Coast to speak with a major connect since it was mandatory that the head of the crew, who was his best friend Laron, be there. That trip saved his life, at the same time he couldn't help but think that maybe if he had been there, the men that he considered to be his family might still be alive.

"We need to go," Clip's bodyguard said, not wanting to disturb his boss but he also knew it was time. "We don't want to be late getting to the airport."

Clip nodded his head and stood silently for a few more minutes before heading towards the awaiting limo. "Chuck, let's go to the airport," he said once he got inside. "This can't wait any longer. We have work to do."

Chapter 5
CHARGE IT TO THE GAME

"Yo, this clown love makin' motherfuckers wait," Deion said through clenched teeth.

"Yeah, he definitely 'bout that bullshit," Bernard said from the backseat, lying down. "It's uncomfortable as a motherfucker back here."

"I think this him right now," Deion said, answering the unknown number. "Yo."

"You got my money?"

"Right here," Deion said, looking over at the charcoal leather duffel bag on the passenger seat.

"Drive to that restaurant across the street," the man said, then hung up.

"Give them boys the heads up we going to that

restaurant across the street," Deion stated, starting the ignition. "As soon as that nigga get this money and we get Passion and Demonte, tell 'em to kill his ass."

When Deion pulled in the parking lot, his eyes darted around looking for any suspicious activities, but there was nothing but parked cars. Right when Deion was about to turn off his headlights, he saw somebody coming towards him wearing a hoodie and sweatpants.

"Here he come. I might kill this nigga right now my damn self."

"Hold on, we gotta get yo' girl and her kid first," Bernard reminded Deion.

"I know. I'm just talkin' shit. Hold up a minute," Deion said, leaning forward."

"What's wrong... it ain't him?"

"Nah, it ain't him. It's Passion," Deion said, unlocking the door. "What you doin' here and where's Demonte?" he questioned when Passion got in the car.

"He made me come get the money."

"Why?"

"He said in case you tried anything slick, like tryna kill him. He put me in the trunk and drove me here and left me with the car. He said to get the money from you and once I did he would call and tell me where to bring it."

"That slick fuck. What about Demonte?"

"He still got Demonte. He said if I wanted my son back I better do everything he say."

"Damn!" Deion barked, pounding his fist on the steering wheel. "This must be him right now."

"Give yo' girl the money and don't you follow her."

"I ain't givin' her shit until you give me Demonte. How I know you ain't gon' take the money then kill both of them?"

"Don't play wit' me, nigga!"

"The only one playin' is you."

"When she get back to the car wit' the money and drives off, I'll give you the boy. Once all the money is accounted for then I'll tell you where you can pick yo' girl up. Take it or leave it. But if you leave it, the boy is dead."

Deion wanted to reach through the phone and

rip the motherfucker's tongue out his mouth but he had to play it cool. He could live with a lot of shit but being responsible for Demonte's death wasn't one of them. "She coming now, so bring Demonte."

"Deion, if he kills me just please, please take care of my son for me," Passion pleaded.

"Ain't nobody gon' kill you," Deion said, stroking the side of Passion's face. "I'ma work this out. Now go 'head so we can get you and Demonte home." Deion handed Passion the duffel bag full of money and watched her walk towards the car.

"You want the men to make a move?"

"Have two cars follow Passion but make sure they keep they distance. If we get Demonte back, I can't have that boy grow up without his mother. So don't have them do anything that might get her killed. I want my money back but if I have to lose it in order to keep Passion alive, then I'll just have to charge it to the game."

"Got you," Bernard said, calling up his men.

Deion was becoming impatient waiting to see Demonte. It had only been a couple of minutes but it felt like forever to him. He imagined how scared he had to be and wanted the boy back. Deion remembered being afraid as a child and no one protecting him. Those were painful memories he wanted to bury, but he couldn't. The notion of Demonte or any other child experiencing that sort of fear fucked with Deion's psyche. His mind was so preoccupied that at first Deion didn't hear the loud scream. But after the second time, he was shook out of his thoughts.

"Uncle Deion! Uncle Deion!" Deion jumped out of his car and Demonte came running towards him. He held onto Deion tightly. "I'm so glad you came and got me. I wanna go home." Deion picked Demonte up and carried him to the car.

"They lost her," Bernard said when Deion got back in the car.

"Is he talking about my mommy?" Demonte asked with his eyes watering up.

"No, he's talking about someone else. Come on, I'ma take you home. Are you hungry? You want something to eat?"

"Can we go to Baskin-Robbins? I want some ice cream."

"You got it," Deion said, rubbing the top of Demonte's head. He then eyed Bernard and mouthed *find her* before driving off.

Chapter 6
Eye For An Eye

"I can't lie. I've missed you, Alex, please come in."
Isabella smiled, extending her arm and welcoming
Alex into her hotel suite at the Four Seasons in
Atlanta.

"You look beautiful as always." Alex smiled
back, taking a seat on one of the couches.

"I have to be honest. I'm happy you're back, but
I didn't think it would be so soon," Isabella admitted,
pouring herself a glass of champagne. "Would you
like some?" she offered.

"No, thank you."

"So why the change? A couple of months ago
you said you were done with this business. You were

getting married, starting a family, and wanted to live your life completely legal. Does your wife have expensive taste like me and run through all your money," Isabella joked.

"Actually, I never had a chance to get married."

"What… you called off the engagement?"

"No, my fiancé was brutally murdered."

"Alex, I'm so sorry. I feel embarrassed over the insensitive joke I just made."

"No need to apologize. I know you meant no harm."

"Do you know who killed her?"

"Yes, and I've made sure that they've paid dearly."

"I wouldn't expect anything less from you. The pain of loss love can be almost unbearable but at least you've experienced real love and you will fall in love again… I promise you."

"I seriously doubt that, Isabella, and you know what?"

"What?"

"I don't want to. I can't go through this again. I loss Dahlia and our child; I'm not built to endure that sort of pain twice. I'm barely surviving now. That's why I need to get back to work. Keep my mind occupied."

"I understand and you're in luck. Sources tell me there is a serious drought in some parts. A major supplier, probably your only competition in the area, is out of business."

"Is that right," Alex said, not letting on that he knew exactly what she was talking about because he was responsible for putting them out of commission.

"Yes. I'm sure you've heard of Get Money Crew."

"No doubt."

"Clearly they pissed off the wrong people because the entire organization has been wiped out. With them no longer in business that leaves you open to take over their territories."

"I can handle that if you can meet the demand."

"Alex, darling, don't offend me. I'll supply you with so much heroin you'll be able to retire a wealthy man by the end of this year if you like."

"You can pour me that glass of champagne now, 'cause we need to toast to that."

"Say no more." Isabella beamed.

Deion was about to go crazy as he paced back and forth in his apartment. It had been three days and still no word on Passion. He didn't have a number on the kidnapper and he had made no attempt to contact him since Passion left with the money. What was bothering Deion even more was he didn't know what to tell Demonte. He was just a little boy and all he knew was that he was back home but his mother wasn't. He was staying with his grandmother and she seemed like a nice woman but she wouldn't be able to replace his mother. Deion had his men and a private investigator looking for Passion. If she were alive, he would bring her home, but if she was dead… Deion put his head down getting stressed out even thinking about it.

"Hello," Deion answered his cell phone, ready to have a strong drink at nine o'clock in the morning.

"I think I might have a lead," Tony, the private investigator informed Deion. "Can I come over? I want to show you some photos I took."

"Yeah, come now. I'll be waitin' for you."

"Great, I'll be there shortly." Before Deion even hung up with Tony, he saw that Bernard was beeping on the other line.

"What you got for me?"

"Man, we still ain't got nothing."

"Then why you calling me?" Deion asked with an attitude while slipping on some sweats and a t-shirt before the private investigator showed up.

"I was calling about the Get Money Crew."

"What about 'em? They all dead."

"Some of my lil' niggas that be keeping they ears to the streets been hearing that people are saying you and Alex are responsible for that hit."

"And..."

"That folks might be looking for retribution."

"Who gives a fuck. Ain't nobody left in that crew to carry that shit out."

"Maybe some of they family members. You know how niggas be."

"First of all, can't nobody prove we had anything to do wit' that hit. But say somebody can prove it, don't nobody want it wit' us. We run ATL. If a joker out here wanna get got, we got something for 'em. Get word on the street that if we even think somebody tryna bring heat our way, we shootin' first and ain't askin' no questions. You heard?"

"Yeah, yeah. I'll make sure that shit spread swiftly. I got you covered."

"Good, but I gotta go," Deion said, hearing somebody at his front door, who he assumed was Tony. "I'll hit you later, but call me if you get any word on Passion."

"Will do."

Deion ended his call with Bernard and quickly went to get the door. He was anxious to see the photos Tony had. "What's good man," Deion said, letting Tony in.

"I know you're a busy man so I'm going to get right to it," Tony said, handing Deion a manila envelope. Deion appreciated him jumping straight to business because he really didn't have time or interest in small talk.

Deion sat down on the couch and went through the photos. His jaw began to flutter as his eyes studied each image.

"From the license plate number you gave me I was finally able to track down the car. Do you know a Trina McDonald?"

"Nah, I can't say that I do."

"Well the car is registered in her name. But when I went to the address that was on the registration, this Ms. McDonald person no longer lives there."

"When were these pictures taken?"

"Last night. I know it's dark outside, but you can clearly see that it's your girlfriend."

"That sneaky bitch," Deion mumbled, tossing the pics on the table. There was no denying that was Passion getting out of the car. She was dressed in the same hoodie and sweatpants she had on when he gave her the bag of money. "Did you see anybody else with her?"

"No. I saw her go into that house and she never came back out. I didn't see anybody else come in or out either and I sat out there all night. Do you want me to keep watching the house?"

"Nah, I'll take it from here. Just give me all the

information you have," Deion said, getting up and retrieving his wallet. "This should be more than enough to cover all your expenses," he said, handing the private investigator some money.

"This is everything, including the home address where she's staying," he said, handing Deion another envelope. "If you need me to handle anything else for you, let me know," Tony said, before leaving.

Deion breathed heavily, sitting back down and analyzing the pictures again. The more he studied the pics the more enraged he became. Everything Deion did was to make sure Demonte wouldn't have to grow up without his mother. Now Deion would be the one responsible for taking Demonte's mother away. Because there was no question in Deion's mind that Passion had to go, and he would be the one to put the bullet in her.

Chapter 7
GIVE UP THE GOODS

"Who the fuck can that be," Deion muttered out loud, putting his gun in the back of his pants. "Who is it?" he said loudly, walking towards the door.

"It's me, Alex."

"My man, what you doing here?" Deion said, giving Alex dap.

"I was in your area and wanted to come speak to you for a minute. Did I catch you at a bad time?" Alex questioned, noticing Deion was dressed in all black and seemed to be in a hurry."

"I always got time for my best friend and partner."

"Man, I've known you damn near all my life

and I can tell when you up to no good. Tell me what's really going on."

"I don't want you caught up in my bullshit. The less you know the better."

"Fuck that, you my brother. If something going on wit' you I want to know. This mood you in, does it have anything to do with Passion?"

"Yeah," Deion acknowledged, biting down on his bottom lip. "That bitch played me. She the one that set up the kidnapping. That ho think she two hundred and fifty thousand dollars richer."

"Are you serious? These broads out here can be so scandalous. You can't trust none of them," Alex said, shaking his head.

"Who you tellin' and I thought she was one of the good ones. But I did get her ass from the strip club so what the fuck should I expect. I think why I'm so surprised is 'cause she used her son to make it happen. I never thought she would do no foul shit like that. Demonte be calling me every day asking me have I found his mommy yet."

"Damn, that poor kid."

"Tell me about it. How I'ma tell that boy his

mama dead."

"Deion, you gon' kill her?" Alex asked.

"Hell the fuck yeah. You think I'ma let that snake ho run off wit' my money. You already know she got to go."

"I feel you but what about her son?"

"She shoulda thought about that before she plotted on my paper."

"True," Alex reasoned.

"But I'll make sure Demonte straight. That's my lil' man. He'll be taken care of."

"I don't care how well you provide for that kid, it ain't gon' replace his mother."

"Don't you think I know that better than anybody? As fucked up as my mom's was, I still would've given anything to have her in my life."

Alex went quiet not knowing how to respond. He knew Deion's mother was a touchy subject and he didn't want to make his friend feel any more fucked up than he already was. Instead of going deeper into what would turn into a painful conversation, Alex decided to switch topics. "With GMC no longer in business, their territories are wide open for the taking."

"You right but I don't think we can get our hands on enough product to supply every spot they left behind."

"I was concerned about that too but I met with Isabella and she said it wouldn't be a problem."

"Word?" Deion questioned with a raised eyebrow. "That's a whole lot of drugs. I believe my coke connect can up my load by some, but I would need Isabella to give us some of that, too. Can she?"

"Yep," Alex nodded.

"Man, if we take over GMC's territory we'll be unstoppable," Deion said, smiling at the thought.

"Is that a grin I see on yo' face," Alex joked, glad to see that Deion's frown was now a smile.

"Yeah man. You know makin' mo' money always put a smile on my face. Shit, ain't that what we in this game for, to make as much fuckin' money as possible."

"No doubt. If we gon' do this, we need to move now. We don't wanna wait and give some other crew an opportunity to come in and take over."

"I agree. Let me take care of this Passion

situation and I'm ready to dive in head first."

"Cool. But be careful wit' that. I need you out on these streets wit' me and not locked up."

"Never that." Deion laughed, play punching Alex in the arm. "But damn, man, I'm glad you back in the game. I knew eventually you would come around, but not so soon."

"It may sound crazy, but I get strength from these streets. They give me power."

"That don't sound crazy at all. I feel the same way. We in this together so we both got the power," Deion stated as the men clutched hands.

Deion, Bernard, and two of his workers sat in a tinted minivan up the street from the house where Passion was staying. It was a nondescript one-story home on the outskirts of Atlanta. They had been watching the place for the last couple of hours and there hadn't been any activity until about fifteen minutes ago. A burgundy Jeep Cherokee pulled into the garage but they weren't able to get a clear view of who was inside, but it looked to be a man. The Maxima that Passion had been driving when she picked up the money was also parked out front but there was no sign of her. Deion assumed she was inside and he was ready to make his move.

"Ya'll ready?" he asked, putting on his ski mask and grabbing his AR-15.

"Yep, we ready," Bernard responded, answering for the other men. They followed Deion's lead, putting on the ski masks and retrieving their weapons also.

"Bernard you come through the front with me; you two take the back. When I give the signal, we kicking doors in and you know what to do next," Deion ordered, as everyone got out the minivan and headed towards the house. It was dark outside. The street was dimly lit and they were dressed all in black, making it easy for the foursome to go unnoticed.

As Deion stood outside the front door, he could hear the television, but no other voices. On the sly he peeped his head through the window and saw the back of a man's head sitting in front of the television. "This nigga ain't gon' know what hit 'im,"

Deion mumbled, before giving the whistle signal to kick in the door.

"Put yo' motherfuckin' hands up or I'ma blow yo' head off," Deion roared, aiming the lightweight rifle at the back of the man's head.

"We looked around, nobody else is here," one of the men said, coming from the back with their guns raised.

"Man what ya want? I ain't got no money. You wanna take my flat screen, you can," the man said with his hands still raised.

"Nigga, don't nobody want yo' tv," Deion said, still not making face-to-face contact with the man, but feeling that something seemed familiar about him. "What the fuck is yo' name?" Deion questioned, walking towards him. Once Deion was standing in front of the man he took the tip of his gun and slammed it against his temple.

"What tha fuck!" the man screamed in pain, holding his hand over the gash on his head as blood poured out. "Take whatever you want. Ain't no need for all this," he wailed.

Deion took his ski mask off slowly, wanting

the man to see his face before he was tortured and killed. "Nigga, I shoulda killed you the first time," Deion spit, ready to gouge out his eyes.

"Deion, man, I paid you back yo' money, why you doing this?"

"Yeah, you paid me back my money and then turned around and stole my two hundred and fifty g's. I shoulda had you murked when Travis was taken care of. But I won't make that mistake again. After I kill you, I'ma hunt Trina down and make sure she dead and Passion too for being in on this bullshit. What them hoes friends or something? How long ya plotted on this shit? Was it ever since I met Passion at the strip club? I need names, 'cause everyone involved is dead," Deion said, stomping his boot in Terrance's stomach. "So you betta gets to talkin'. Ain't no sense in you dying alone."

"Man, I don't know what you talkin' bout'. I ain't stole no money from you and I don't know nobody named Passion. I swear. This a misunderstanding."

"So that's yo' story."

"It ain't no story, it's the truth."

"Have it yo' way. I'ma find Trina and Passion

anyway. Both them bitches dead. I hope they enjoyin' that money, 'cause where they goin', they ain't gonna be able to take it wit' 'em," Deion stated before blasting three bullets in Terrance, hitting his neck, chest, and stomach. Deion watched as the hot led balls ripped through his skin, killing him instantly. "This nigga wasn't even worth torturing. Check around and make sure my money ain't stashed here before we bounce and hurry up 'cause I'm sick of looking at the motherfucker."

Deion sat down and lit a cigarette while he waited for his men to do their search. He needed to calm his nerves. Deion was still stunned that Passion had partnered up with Terrance to rob him. It made his stomach turn thinking that all these months Passion had been working him. He had even developed a soft spot for her son and the entire time she was scheming with Terrance and Trina. Killing Passion was going to be Deion's ultimate hard on, he thought to himself.

"Deion, come here. There's something you need to see," Bernard hollered. Deion put out his cigarette on the table and headed towards his men.

Chapter 8
THE START OF YOUR ENDING

"Thanks for coming with me to get something to eat," Reggie said as he and Alex were seated at a table at Tantra on Peachtree Rd.

"You didn't leave me much of a choice. You driving and basically refused to drop me at my crib before you came here."

"True, but you need to get out."

"What you talkin' about. I have gotten out."

"I'm talkin' besides work. You know, to relax, have a good meal. I know it's gonna take some time for you to stop hurting over Dahlia, but I think gettin' back out here will do you good."

"If only it was that easy. Work is the only thing

keeping me grounded right now."

"Have you heard back from that caller?"

"Nah. I think you might've been right. It was just a hoax, man. I got myself worked up thinking I had another score to settle but we killed the right people. GMC was responsible and now it's time for me to move on."

"I hope you mean that, man, 'cause I want you to be..." Reggie stopped mid-sentence when someone caught his eye.

"What you looking at?" Alex asked, turning in the direction Reggie was staring.

"Reggie, Alex, hi." Tierney smiled, coming to their table. "How are you doing?" Tierney asked, turning her attention to Alex.

"I'm good and you?"

"Great... I heard about your girlfriend."

"She was my fiancé."

"Pardon me, your fiancé. I guess it's important for you to remind me that although you didn't think I was good enough, you found someone who was worthy to put a ring on," Tierney mocked.

"Tierney, everything isn't about you and my

relationship with Dahia definitely wasn't. So get over yo'self."

"Listen, I heard about your girlfriend, excuse me, I meant your fiancé and I wanted to come over and give you my condolences. I would've called but I deleted your number a long time ago. But I'm glad you're well and I wish you nothing but the best," she continued. "My friends are waiting for me so I won't keep you any longer. Nice seeing you Reggie." Tierney smiled and walked away.

"Good seeing you, too," Reggie said, before picking up his menu. "That was awkward." Reggie laughed.

"I guess that's one way of putting it," Alex said, getting a good laugh out of it, too. "Who would've thought having a conversation with Tierney would put me in a good mood."

"Does that mean you still interested in her?" Reggie inquired.

"That would be a negative. Been there and never wanna go back but it was fun gettin' under her skin. That's what put me in a good mood."

"Whatever works. I just want my friend back.

Having you around balances out Deion."

"Deion ain't that bad."

"I got mad love for Deion but we both know he always one step away from blowin' some shit up. With you always in his ear keeps him from jumping all the way off the edge."

"Yeah, I just know Deion better than anyone else... what makes him tic and how to diffuse a situation before it gets too out of control. But under all the aggression and craziness, he a good dude."

"You right, he is and there is no denying he would do anything for you. That nigga love you like a brother fo' real."

"The feeling is mutual. Now let's eat," Alex said, putting down his menu and signaling the waitress to come over and take their order.

"Where ya at?" Deion questioned, not seeing his men.

"We up here in the attic." Deion noticed an opening by the closet and went up the stairs. Deion's eyes widened in shock when he reached the top of the stairs. "Yo, cover her up," Deion barked when he saw Passion.

"Outta respect, we didn't want to touch her without you seeing her first. Sorry, boss," Bernard explained.

There wasn't a blanket or anything to put over Passion so Deion took off his black hoodie and placed it over her naked body. It broke his heart to see Passion's badly beaten and bruised body handcuffed to a makeshift pole. She seemed so lifeless that at first Deion didn't even know if she was alive. He thought she might be dead but heard her slightly breathing, yet barely holding on.

"Passion, bae, wake up," he said, stroking her face as he cradled her limp body. "Go find the fuckin' key! Hurry up!"

"Go check and see if he got some keys in his pocket," Bernard told one of the men. "You go get a blanket," he said to the other guy.

"Passion, you gotta hold on. You can't die. Demonte need you. Don't make me tell that boy his mother not coming back," he pleaded.

Passion's eyes were so beaten and blackened that they were swollen shut. She was lying on a bloody mattress thrown in the middle of the floor. Terrance had Passion stashed in the attic like a brutalized slave. All the hatred Terrance had for Deion he unleashed it on an innocent and helpless Passion.

"What tha' fuck is takin' so long. Where's the fuckin' key! Deion belted, becoming more and more frustrated.

"I'll go check," Bernard said, hurrying down the stairs. He was very familiar with that look Deion had in his eyes, and there was a real possibility that he might just start randomly shooting motherfuckers if they were in striking distance.

"Hold on, baby. I'ma get you outta here," Deion kept saying over and over again until he finally heard his men coming up the stairs.

"Sorry it took so long but the key was in the kitchen," the worker explained.

"Just give me the fuckin' key," Deion said, grabbing it out of his hand. Bernard then handed him a blanket. "Bring the minivan to the front," he directed. "I'ma get you to the hospital. I need you to stay strong. Demonte needs you," Deion whispered in Passion's ear. He wrapped her body in the blanket before carrying her downstairs to the awaiting car.

Chapter 9
THE SURVIVAL OF THE FITTEST

"Fuck, you look like shit," Alex said when Deion opened the door.

"That's to be expected since I ain't slept in forty-eight hours," Deion responded, letting Alex inside his apartment.

"What happened?"

"I've been at the hospital the last couple of days. I just got back home so I could get some sleep, shower, and change clothes," Deion explained, falling back on the couch, barely able to keep his eyes open.

"Hospital? Is you hurt... somebody else hurt? Talk to me."

"It's Passion. She's in pretty bad shape."

"Wait, I'm confused. Last time we talked you were on your way to kill Passion for settin' you up. Now you lookin' devastated that she in the hospital, so I'm assuming it wasn't you that put her there."

"Nah, it wasn't me. I was wrong, Alex, and I feel like shit."

"Wrong about what?"

"It wasn't Passion that set me up, it was Terrance."

"Terrance?" Alex questioned as his mind scrambled trying to figure out who Deion was talking about. "You ain't talkin' 'bout Tee is you?"

"I sure am," Deion said, nodding his head. "That foul nigga set me up."

"He was still pissed at you for shootin' him in the ass and slicing his girl's face? Damn, Deion." Alex shook his head.

"I know and Passion got caught up in the middle of my bullshit. He had her chained up, so badly beaten I thought she was dead."

Alex's mouth dropped before saying, "What! I didn't even think soft ass Tee had it in him to do something that diabolical."

"Me neither. That's why he never crossed my

mind as being behind the set up. I didn't think he had the balls."

"Is Passion gonna make it?"

"Yeah, thank goodness."

"Thank goodness is right."

"Who you tellin'. I would be sick right now if I had to go to that woman's house and tell her mom that her daughter was dead and tell Demonte his mother ain't comin' home."

"When is she gettin' out the hospital?"

"They want to keep her for a few more days. But she's awake and I got to talk to her for a little while before she went back to sleep."

"What did she say?"

"She said she was sorry. Can you believe that? She blamed herself."

"Sorry for what?"

"That she didn't call me. That night the private investigator saw her, Terrance had sent her out to buy some shit, but he was just testing her, fuckin' wit her, playin' mind games. He threatened her saying he knew where her mom lived and would kill Demonte if she tried to get help and didn't do exactly what he said. That very night he beat her, handcuffed, and..." Deion's voice cracked before he could finish.

"And what?" Alex wanted to know.

"Raped her."

Alex put his head down after Deion disclosed that information. He could only imagine how hard this was on Passion and when, if ever, she would be able to get over her ordeal. Based on the strained look on Deion's face, Alex highly doubted it.

"I don't even know what to say, Deion, except for at least Passion is still alive. Dahlia was raped but that wasn't enough for them, they had to kill her too. So you luckier than me, 'cause I would do anything to have Dahlia back."

Deion swallowed hard. Listening to what Alex said had him feeling like shit. If Alex knew that it was he, his best friend, that raped and murdered Dahlia, nobody would be able to stop him from killing Deion.

"You right, Passion is alive. I need to be thankful for that. But man, I'm exhausted. I gotta get some sleep."

"I feel you," Alex said, patting Deion's shoulder

before standing up. "If you need anything you know I'm here for you."

"I know and I 'ppreciate that. But I'll be straight. It's Passion who has a long road to recovery, if not physically definitely mentally."

"You right. Is she staying with her mom when she get out?"

"Yeah, you know that townhouse she had blew up in that explosion that Terrance started. Two of Passion's girlfriends were the dead bodies found in her crib."

"So Tee killed Popcorn, too?"

"I'm guessing. But it's hard to believe that silly nigga—who could barely move ounces without trippin' over himself—made all this shit happen on his own."

"I agree, so you betta make sure you continue to watch yo' back. This shit might not be over."

"True and I will, but the first thing I'ma do is work on gettin' a house for Passion and Demonte. The very least I can do is get them a new crib."

"I think that's a good idea. I'm proud of you for even thinkin' of that. That dude Danny I told you about—"

"The white boy?" Deion questioned, cutting Alex off.

"Yep. He works in real estate. He was the one that got me that house that I planned on moving into with Dahlia and our baby..." Alex said, as his voice trailed off. "But umm, he can find something for you."

"Yeah, call him for me. I wanna move on that ASAP."

"Will do. Take your time handling your personal situation. When you ready we can get back to business."

"Thank you. Love you, bro."

"Love you, too," Alex said, as the two men gave each other a brotherly hug. After Alex left, the first thing Deion did was call Bernard.

"I was just about to hit you up," were the first words out of Bernard's mouth when he answered the phone. "I got that address."

"Good. You go kill Trina and anybody else in that crib. Don't leave nobody alive. But make sure you try to find out where my money is first. Don't waste no whole bunch of time tryna get it out of her though. Your main objective is to kill. Call me when ya done. If I don't answer, leave a message."

Deion tossed his phone down before heading to his bedroom to take a shower and go to sleep.

Chapter 10
No Discipline

6 Months Later...

"Damn, Reggie, you got it looking like Vegas up in this motherfucker. Impressive." Deion grinned when he stepped into the VIP section of the newly renovated lounge. "This must've cost a pretty penny."

"You should know since you paid for it." Reggie laughed.

"Word. It's nice to see my money was well spent," Deion commented, looking around the lounge. The illuminated white walls ushered you down two entries that lead you to the main room or VIP seating on the back wall. Off to the side was a staircase to a glass-enclosed hallway that wraps above one of the bars leading to an outside patio. The décor was a metropolitan flair, inspired by an Italian villa; paintings, chandeliers and fine marble tiles. "This place is fuckin' beautiful."

"Yeah, it is," Reggie said, walking over to Deion and standing next to him. "You should be proud to be a partner."

"I am," Deion said, looking out into the crowd over the balcony. "This place is big enough to be a club, you know."

"Yeah, but I think a lounge gives it a more intimate, mature, sexy vibe."

"You right. This opening definitely brought out all the grown and sexy women tonight. I mean damn, I'm seeing one bad bitch after another," Deion said.

"You ain't lyin'. If I knew there would be so many chicks to choose from I wouldn't of brought a date."

"That's yo' dumbass fault. Why you would bring a date to a highly anticipated re-opening of this lounge is beyond me. But I ain't complaining. It just gives me more hoes to choose from," Deion said.

"Since you on the prowl, I guess that means Passion ain't coming."

"Nah, but she ain't even in town. She took Demonte to Disney World wit' her mom."

"That's nice. I know lil' man is loving that."

"Yeah he is." Deion smiled. "It's his first time going. He's a good kid and he had a rough few months so he deserves the trip."

"You really like him, don't you," Reggie stated.

"I do. He's like the son I never had."

"Wow, you talkin' 'bout having kids."

"That's not what I said."

"Then what are you saying?"

"I think I'm in love."

"Huh? You in love wit' Passion?"

"No, with the woman that just walked through the front door," Deion said, not taking his eyes off of her.

"You gotta be talking about the woman in that gold dress. Wow, she is gorgeous. I can't even lie."

"I thought I had ran across every dime in ATL but I ain't neva seen that face and body before. I wouldn't forget her."

"I haven't either. Maybe she new to town."

"Maybe so, but I'm about to find out," Deion said, before he headed in the woman's direction. The woman was now sitting at the lower level bar, about to order a drink when Deion walked up.

"Whatever she's having I'll pay for it." The woman turned around in her barstool to see who was offering to buy her drink.

"I appreciate the gesture but that's not necessary. I can buy my own drink."

"I don't doubt that. I would just like to buy it for you."

"What's your name?" she asked.

"Deion."

"Deion, clearly you're a very confident man, but I'm here with my girlfriend just trying to have a good time. I'm not really in the mood to entertain a man right now."

"Oh, I get it. So you a lesbian."

"Not that sort of girlfriend."

Before Deion could respond, a woman came walking up to them. "Girl, the line to the bathroom was too long, so I said forget it," she said, taking a seat next to the woman Deion had been talking to.

"I figured that. I was about to order a drink, you want something?" she offered.

"Yeah, get me a Moscato."

"I offered to get your girlfriend a drink. I'd like to extend the same offer to you."

"Hold up," the girl said, raising her hand. "Isn't your name Deion?"

"Yeah, why? I know you?"

"You used to mess with a girlfriend of mine. You fucked her a couple of times then you stopped returning her phone calls. Yeah, you the one. I remember you. You a dog."

"No disrespect but one indiscretion with yo' girlfriend doesn't make me a dog."

The girl rolled her eyes and took her Moscato. "Save all that suave talk. Kimberly already put me on to you."

"Kimberly... you talkin' 'bout Kimberly that goes to Spellman?"

"Bingo and you know you did her dirty," the girl said, smacking her lips. "Calleigh, I hope you not checkin' for him, 'cause he's a dog."

"Can you chill? All I want to do is have a conversation with your friend. No need in you shittin' on my name before I even have a chance to properly introduce myself."

"Whatever... go 'head," the girl said frowning.

"Calleigh, that's your name right?"

"Yes."

"I think you are absolutely gorgeous and I would love to take you out for dinner, lunch, brunch, or whatever you have available."

"Thanks but no thanks. Like I said, I'm just out with my girlfriend trying to have a good time."

"I respect that. But if you change your mind," Deion said, picking her cell up from off the bar, "Put my number in your phone."

"I won't be changing my mind," she said, snatching her phone out of Deion's hand. "Now if you can excuse us, please," she said, turning towards her girlfriend and talking to her as if Deion was no longer standing there.

Deion wasn't sure if he was angry, offended, or embarrassed by how the woman dismissed him. He walked back over to the VIP section not sure what just happened and how it happened to him. Deion was used to always getting the girl he wanted and this one would be no different.

"So when's the date? 'Cause I know you got them digits." Reggie grinned as Deion sat down.

"She turned me down."

"What?" Reggie questioned, as if not believing him.

"I know. I can't believe it myself, but you know me, I don't take no for an answer."

"So what you gon' do?"

"Not sure yet, but I'll figure it out and soon, 'cause I ain't lettin' shorty get away," Deion said, more as a promise to himself as he stared at her from across the room.

"Hmmmmm, this dick feels so good," Isabella moaned as Alex's rock-hard dick went deeper inside of her. Her pussy kept tightening around his thick tool making Alex thrust harder and harder. He then slowed down grabbing onto Isabella's thick thighs while his tongue licked her erect nipples causing her to go into a frenzy. Isabella's pussy got wetter and wetter as Alex sucked and fucked her at the same time. Isabella stared at Alex with lust in her eyes as her body shivered from her orgasm. Her nails latched onto his back as she squeezed his skin unable to take the ecstasy he was bringing to every inch of her. Her screams turned into a soft cry as Alex kept stroking her wet walls with a steady pace as she reached her second orgasm.

"I love you," Isabella cried out, totally oblivious to anything but how much pleasure Alex was bringing her. Within a few minutes Alex could no longer hold back and he managed to cum so hard, every muscle in his body seemed to collapse.

"Damn, that was good," Alex said, rolling over on his back before taking a deep breath.

"You were amazing," Isabella purred, sprinkling kisses on his neck. "We really do make a great team," she continued as she circled the tip of her freshly manicured nail over each crevice of Alex's chiseled chest. "We could be an unstoppable power couple."

"Except you're already on a team, Isabella... his name is Joaquin and he's your husband," Alex said, getting out of the bed.

"You don't have a bad angle do you," Isabella remarked, watching his six-four solid frame walk towards the bathroom. "Even from the back, you turn me on." Isabella got out of the bed and followed Alex into the bathroom. He was already in the shower and she joined him. "I couldn't stay away," she said lathering his wet body with soap.

"Isabella, what we got is good but we can't..." Alex couldn't finish his sentence when the sensation of Isabella's mouth swallowing his dick had him leaning back against the shower with his eyes closed. The sex with Isabella was always excellent, but part of Alex hated himself for giving into his urges and rekindling a sexual relationship with her. That was never his intention, but Isabella preyed on the vulnerable state Alex was in. She was a woman that knew what she wanted and when the right opportunity presented itself, she couldn't resist making her move.

Now Isabella had even bigger ambitions. She wanted Alex to be her man. That meant having him exclusively. Although she was a married woman, that wasn't a problem for Isabella, simply a minor hitch that would be resolved with a quickie divorce. In her mind, her marriage had been over a long time ago, but if Joaquin wanted to make things difficult for her, murder was always another option.

Chapter 11
LET THE GAMES BEGIN

"Uncle Deion, we had the most fun at Disney World." Demonte beamed, showing Deion the souvenirs and pictures they brought back from the trip.

"That's what's up lil' man. Glad you enjoyed yourself," Deion said, tossing Demonte up in the air, then letting him jump on his shoulders like he loved to do.

"The both of you are so silly." Passion laughed, clearing the food off the table from the dinner she and Demonte just ate. "Enough of that playing around, it's time for you to take a bath and get ready for bed."

"Can I play my Xbox... please?" Demonte begged

as Deion put him down.

"One game, that's it. Then it's bath time."

"Okay!"

Deion smiled as Demonte ran up the stairs to his bedroom. "He really is a great kid," Deion said, walking over to Passion in the kitchen and cupping her ass before giving her a kiss.

"Thank you. While we were away I was thinking how nice it would be for him to have a little brother or sister. What do you think?"

"I think I'ma have a piece of that red velvet cake you made."

Passion folded her arms. "Is that your way of saying no?" She stood silently for a few seconds waiting for Deion's response but instead he took the knife and cut a slice of cake without saying a word. "Deion, I've never made it a secret I want another child. Plus, you put me and Demonte in this big ass house, don't you think I need to start filling it up?"

"The size of a house I bought you shouldn't be a determining factor on whether or not you should have more kids."

"Then how about the fact that I love you and I

want us to have a child together."

"Passion, why you doing this?"

"Doing what, having a conversation with you about our future together."

"Is that what this is about. You tryna secure yo' future."

"I see you still look at me as some low budget on loan stripper. I guess I'm good enough for you to fuck but not make a baby with."

Deion could see Passion's eyes watering up and he hated for her to be pain. Ever since he found her knocking on death's door, the soft spot he had for her son, he also now had for Passion. But that wasn't enough for Deion to be in love with Passion or even tame his dick slinging. He did have love for her but he wasn't in love. At this point in their relationship, Deion felt the main reason he kept it going was because he harbored guilt for what Terrance put her through.

"Baby, it's not like that. I don't look at you as no low budget nothing. I don't care that you used to be a stripper. I mean damn, we both know the type of shit I'm into. I ain't got no room to judge no motherfuckin' body."

"Then if it's not about me being an ex-stripper, then what? Is it because of the..." Passion's voiced cracked as she began getting choked up. "The rape?" She hated for that word to come out her mouth. Understandably, that nightmare she endured was fresh in her mind and her healing process was still in the fragile stages.

"Never that, baby," Deion stated, embracing Passion; giving her the hug she desperately needed. The tears began falling as she held on tightly to him. Deion had never been close to a woman or seen one this vulnerable since he was a little boy and was a witness to it through his mother. The emotions it was stirring up inside of him, scared Deion. He then wondered if this was payback and/or a punishment for what he had done to Alex's fiancé, Dahlia.

"Mommy, I'm ready to take my bath," Demonte yelled out from upstairs, interrupting the sweet, yet tense, moment between them.

"Here I come," Passion replied, still holding on to Deion. "You know I love you," she said in a soft tone. "I just want us—"

"Shh," Deion said, cutting her off. "We can talk about this later. Go upstairs and take care of Demonte. I have some business to deal with but I'll be back over later on tonight," he said, kissing Passion on the forehead.

"Okay."

As Passion was headed upstairs, Deion felt his phone vibrating. He checked to see who was calling him and it was Kimberly. He had left her a message a few days ago, but he really wasn't expecting her to return his call. Deion grabbed his car keys and hurried out the front door to his car, not wanting Passion to hear him take the call.

"What up, Kimberly. I wasn't sure I would hear back from you, but I'm glad you called."

"Oh, is it because of how you played me? We had sex, then you basically kicked me out your crib, but said you were going to call me the next day because you were taking me to the Rihanna concert for my birthday. You never called and then I see yo' ass at the concert with some other bitch."

"Yeah about that. I felt really bad. I wanted to make it up to you."

"Make it up to me how?"

"I know I'm late, but I have a birthday present for you."

"Really?" the girl smacked, not convinced. "What kind of present, 'cause if it's some dick you can keep it."

"Nothing like that." Deion laughed, keeping his cool. "Trust me, it's worth your time to come get it."

"I guess. So are you going to bring it to me? How is this gonna work?"

"Come by this lounge I own and get it. I'll text you the address. I'm on my way there now."

"Don't be bullshttin' me, Deion."

"Kimberly, I got you. See you soon."

Clip had been staying in an undisclosed location in the outskirts of Atlanta since the Get Money Crew had been wiped out. Only a few key people knew that he was even alive and his whereabouts. Clip hadn't been able to conduct any business, but luckily for him, he had made more than enough millions to sit down and basically become a ghost for the last few months. If he wanted to find out who was responsible for murdering his entire crew and why, he had no choice. Clip couldn't front, he missed the hustle and bustle of being out in them streets making moves. The life of crime ran through his blood. At the age of thirteen, he was already a young boss, running product on the blocks of projects. To sit still was almost like a death sentence to him, but he was willing to do it, all for the love of his brothers.

Clip was well aware that if it got out that he had survived the hit, the person or people responsible might come looking for him to finish the job. So he spent his time gathering all the necessary information to plot their demise.

The sound of his cell phone ringing interrupted Clip's thoughts. It was easy for him to become immersed in thinking while sitting outside underneath the pergola that overlooked his private lake. "Hello."

"I wanted you to know that everything is moving forward as planned."

"Excellent. I'll be waiting for the next update.

Thanks, Chuck." A smile crept across Clip's face. "Vengeance will be mine."

Chapter 12
WANT IT ALL

"I'm glad you came." Deion smiled, giving Kimberly a hug and a kiss on the cheek. "Can I get you something to drink, maybe some champagne?"

"I guess some champagne would be nice," Kimberly said, flipping her hair behind her head.

"Go have a seat and I'll have a waitress bring it to you. I'll be over there shortly." Deion laughed to himself as Kimberly tried to give him a sassy attitude and then strutted to her seat. She was wearing an extra tight mini dress that highlighted every curve she had and some most wouldn't know existed. She seemed to be putting on a show for Deion, but he wasn't interested. He had been there and done that. "Karen, give that young lady sitting over there a bottle of our best champagne. Give her whatever else she wants, too. Thanks."

"Whose panties are you tryna get in now?" Reggie joked when he approached Deion.

"Nobody in here."

"Then what's up with the bottle service?"

"Just tryna soften someone up so I can get what I need."

"Nigga, you gon' be a playa for life."

"No doubt. It's too bad Passion don't understand that shit."

"What's going on wit' ya? I thought everything was good over there."

"I did too until she dropped the baby bomb on me."

"You gon' be a daddy? She pregnant?" Reggie asked.

"Nah, but she said she's ready to give Demonte a baby brother or sister."

"And you ain't interested."

"Nope. Honestly I'm not even into her like that no more but I don't wanna hurt her," Deion admitted, putting his head down.

"Let me find out you got a sensitive side. You," Reggie said, pointing at Deion like he was stunned, "you care about a woman being hurt? What the fuck is in yo' drink. I didn't think you really gave a fuck about anybody but the kids and Alex." Reggie laughed but was serious.

"Nigga, fuck you." Deion laughed back, tossing an ice cube from his drink at Reggie. "Let me go deal wit' this chick. I'll talk to you in a minute."

"Good luck," Reggie teased while Deion was walking away.

As Deion got closer to Kimberly he could see that she had already finished almost half the bottle of champagne. "I see you enjoying yourself," Deion said, holding up the bottle.

"Yeah, I love the bubbly and you got me the good stuff too, but where is my birthday present? I don't see no wrapping paper with bows or ribbons anywhere."

"What I'ma give you, you can buy all the bows and ribbons you want," Deion stated, pulling out a wad of money and peeling off ten, one hundred dollar bills. "This is a thousand dollars."

Kimberly's eyes widened in delight. "This is for me?"

"Yep."

"And you don't want no pussy?"

"Nope."

"You sure?" Kimberly gave Deion a stare as if letting him know she was more than willing to give him some if he so desired.

"Positive, but I have more of this," Deion said, waving some more hundreds in Kimberly's face, "if you want it."

"Hell yeah, I want it! I'm a struggling college student. I need all the money I can get. So what you want, a threesome or something? I'll do just about anything but transport some drugs. I plan on attending law school so I can't take a chance catching a charge like that. But I'm down for anything else."

"I'm glad you said that."

"So what's up?" she questioned, taking another sip of her champagne as her eyes danced in anticipation at getting ahold of some more of that green paper.

"A girlfriend of yours came here a few nights ago."

"I have several girlfriends. I need a name or description... something."

"I don't know her name but she's a cute brown-skinned girl with a short Toni Braxton-type cut."

"Oh, you must be talking about my girl Dominque. Yeah, her hair be laid. What, you wanna do a threesome with her?"

"I'm not interested in a threesome and I'm not interested in Dominique."

"Then what?"

"I want her friend... Calleigh."

For the first time, Kimberly came up for air and put her champagne glass down on the table, clearly perturbed. "Since that bitch came to town, every time we go out all the niggas be checkin' for her, now you. It's like you all get a new pussy alert or something."

"So how do I get in touch with her?"

"Why should I help you?" she questioned, rolling her eyes.

"Because like you said, you want as much of

this green paper as you can get."

"So you want to buy her phone number from me?"

"Yes, and her address."

"You are so slimy, Deion. You called me, plied me with alcohol and waved money in my face all so you can get next to some woman." Kimberly shook her head. "Obviously you met her, so what, she turned you down?"

"Yes, but I think she just needs a little convincing. Plus, yo' girlfriend Dominique shitted on me all based on the bad mouthing you did."

"Well, you deserved it."

"That might be true, that's why I'm lacing yo' pockets something lovely for the info. Then we can call it even. A win-win for both of us. So what do you say?"

"Start handing over those Benjamin Franklins while I write down the number and address," Kimberly said, reaching in her purse for a pen before writing down the info on a white napkin.

"That shit better be accurate."

"As of yesterday it was. Now hand over the

money," she demanded, rubbing her fingers together.

"Currently we have Washington Street Apartments, Edgewood Center, and Vanira Village on lock. What's the holdup with Santa Fe Villas?" Alex asked his team of workers as they all sat around the round table for their weekly meeting.

"We keep gettin' resistance," one of the workers said.

"What you mean 'resistance'? That was a GMC spot. We were able to get their other locations. So how are you gettin' resistance, they ain't around no more. They all dead."

"I think what Lamont means by resistance is nobody over there is buying our product because somebody else, or another crew, is supplying that area," Bernard explained.

"Well, who the fuck is it?" Alex wanted to know.

"We ain't been able to figure that out."

"You don't see anybody out on the blocks?"

"Nope."

"You think they using one of the units to have buyers come directly there?" Alex questioned.

"We never thought about that."

"Well, you need to figure this shit out."

"Alex, I understand what you sayin', but is it that deep?"

"Excuse me?" Alex asked, like he wasn't sure he heard Lamont correctly.

"All I'm sayin' is besides them three spots we got mad other spots that were left wide open with GMC out the picture. They all bringing in a ton of dough. So it ain't like we need Santa Fe Villas. We straight."

"Who the boss of this shit?"

"You are."

"That means what the fuck I say, go. I say I want Santa Fe Villas. All territory the GMC used to run now belongs to this organization. I want it all. Are we clear?"

The men all nodded their heads in agreement. "We on it boss. You want Santa Fe, we'll get it, that's my word," Bernard promised.

Chapter 13
TEMPTATIONS

Deion was parked across the street from Calleigh's townhouse. He watched as the deliveryman brought her a bouquet of exotic flowers for the seventh day in a row. He was hoping that by now she would've called him to at least say thanks, but she hadn't. She seemed unimpressed. Deion had never been a patient man, but he refused to give up on Calleigh. He wasn't sure if it was because he was extremely attracted to her or was it the challenge of not being able to get her. Deion decided that if he didn't hear from Calleigh by tomorrow then he would implement phase two of his plan.

"Girl, you still not gonna call him?" Dominique asked, smelling the flowers that had just been delivered.

"No," Calleigh replied nonchalantly, sitting back down on the couch, eating her Häagen-Dazs ice cream.

"But why? He is obviously checkin' for you big time. He's been sending you flowers for a week straight. You need to call him."

"Dominique, you are the main one who told me not to fuck with him. Now all of a sudden you want me to call him," Calleigh said, reaching for the remote control to change the channel.

"That was because I didn't want him to dog you out like he did my girl Kimberly. But he's into you. He gave Kimberly like two g's just for your number and address. I had no idea that nigga had paper like that. Probably because he didn't spend none on Kimberly."

"First off, he's not into me because he doesn't even know me. He's into the fact that I ain't chasing after him like all them other chicks he fuck with."

"I'm sure that has a lot to do with it but who cares. Take advantage of that ass. Just let him buy you shit and more shit and even more shit then dump him. But personally, I think you should have sex with him at least one time because that nigga is fine and Kimberly said he can fuck."

"That's another thing. I don't want to date a man Kimberly used to deal with."

"They wasn't dealing with each other per se. He hit it once, twice at the most and dismissed her. I don't think they even went out for dinner, maybe just some takeout."

"Still..."

"Still what?" Dominique said, cutting Calleigh off. "It ain't like Kimberly your bestie. You don't even know her like that. You know her through me."

"True, but we're associates. We've talked on the phone and she's chilled over here a few times."

"Girl please, it ain't that serious, if it was then Kimberly would've never given him your info. She knew what was up."

"Who the fuck gon' turn down two thousand

dollars, especially when you got bills to pay."

"All I'm saying is I think you should give Deion a try. You've been here for a few months now and you haven't dated anybody. I think it's time for you to get some." She giggled.

"Don't worry about my sex life." Calleigh frowned, standing up on her way to the kitchen to toss out her ice cream. As she passed the flowers on the counter she stopped. "They are beautiful, aren't they?"

"They sure are. Seriously Calleigh, what's one date going to hurt?"

"Maybe you're right."

"Does that mean you're going to call him?"

"It means that I'm going to consider it. Now let's get out of here. I just ate all this ice cream, now I need to burn off these calories."

"I bet you could burn a lot of calories off with Deion." Dominique clowned, grabbing her car keys as the ladies headed out.

"My man, Deion, you a hard man to track down," Alex said when Deion stepped through the door of the lounge.

"You know my number, where I live, shit you might be the only motherfucker that know my social security number. So you ain't ever gonna have a problem tracking me down," Deion said, making them all laugh.

"You weren't at the weekly meeting the other day. I was just a little concerned so I thought I would try and catch you before the club opened."

"Didn't Reggie tell you why I wasn't able to make it?" Deion asked, looking over at Reggie.

"Yeah, I told him. You know I be on top of shit."

"Calm down, Reggie." Alex chuckled. "Yeah, he told me you were having some problems with your main coke supplier. Did you get everything worked out?"

"Somewhat, but not really. All of a sudden my fuckin' Mexican connect tryna go up on the prices. After we took over GMC's territory my orders got even bigger. So I'm like, I buy more shit from you than anybody, what the fuck are you doing."

"Listen, I told you before, we can get our coke from Isabella. Fuck that motherfucker if he wanna trip. The more you buy, the lower the prices are supposed to get, not higher."

"Exactly. That's what I told his dumbass, but he know that shit. I told him I can take my business elsewhere and he kinda backed down, but I won't know for sure until I have to re-up. But if he do trip then I'm glad we got Isabella."

"We do and she definitely gonna give us the very best price. I can promise you that," Alex assured him.

"You sound awfully confident, Alex. Is you hittin' that or something?" Reggie smirked.

"Reggie, you know Alex don't kiss and tell. But yeah, he hittin' them skins and I can't blame him. Isabella go in the bad bitch category. But as bad as she is, I might have to pass on that."

"Nigga, shut the hell up! You ain't passing on no prime pussy," Reggie cracked.

"Prime pussy that has a crazy husband attached to it, I would. We all know Joaquin a fool. And you know them types don't play when it comes to their wives. He find out Isabella giving up that pussy to a nigga, he gon' kill her ass."

"Both of ya shut the fuck up. Neither one of you know what my relationship is with Isabella."

"Man, I know you ain't running that shit wit' me," Deion spit. "Listen, I understand your dilemma. I'd be tempted, too, just be careful. We don't wanna have to go to war with Joaquin 'cause you can't keep yo' dick in yo' pants."

"I got everything under control. Don't worry about me. I can handle this," Alex stated assertively. His voice might've sounded confident, but Alex couldn't help but consider what Deion had said. From the moment Isabella made her intentions about him known he tried to resist, mainly because he was doing business with Joaquin. But Isabella was persuasive and Alex gave in. Once he fell in love with Dahlia he thought his sexual relationship with Isabella was a thing of the past, but after her death, Alex found himself going back to familiar territory. Now, he had to admit to himself that things might be getting too deep between them. Isabella had been talking about leaving her husband and them being together as a couple. Alex enjoyed his sexual relationship with Isabella, but he knew it could never be anything more than that as long as Joaquin was alive.

Chapter 14
YOU ALREADY BELONG TO ME

Calleigh was stretched out on the floor in front of her television doing an abs workout. She wasn't an exercise fanatic but she took pride in her curvy yet toned physique and tried her best to maintain it. Since she had a weakness for sweets that meant she had to work out more often than she liked. Right when Calleigh didn't think she could muster enough strength to do another crunch, she heard her doorbell ring and welcomed the interruption.

"Just a minute," she called out on her way to answer the door. When she opened it, Calleigh's eyes widened in shock. She looked around quickly before bending down. "Aren't you gorgeous," she cooed at the snow-white Maltese puppy. The puppy was sitting in a pink Swarovski studded dog throne at her doorstep. "What's your name?" Calleigh held the Maltese up and that's when she saw the diamond tennis bracelet around her neck. "Is this real?" she questioned out loud in disbelief.

"After this, if I can't get you to go out with me then I give up," Deion called out, stepping out of his silver Aston Martin.

"Are these diamonds real?"

"Of course. When I go out, I go all out."

"This puppy is beautiful and this bracelet is gorgeous, but I can't accept this."

"Why not?"

"Because I'm not for sale. It's one thing for you to send me flowers, but this is something else. I know it comes with expectations."

"Just one. Go out with me." Deion was now standing right in front of Calleigh, looking directly in her eyes. She had to admit to herself that he was fine. She didn't remember him being this good-looking but she had seen him in a dimly lit lounge, now he was making his presence known in broad daylight.

"Yes."

"'Yes' what?" He smiled. "I want to hear you say it."

"Yes, I'll go out with you."

"Excellent. I'll pick you up tonight around seven."

"Tonight?"

"Yes, why is that a problem for you?"

"No, tonight is fine."

"Great. I'll see you then, oh and make sure you take good care of the puppy. What are you gonna name her?"

"I told you I'm not keeping her or this bracelet."

"Yes, you are. Name her Diamond because that's what I'm gonna shower you with."

"You love playing games."

"Who said I was playin'. I know what I want. What's wrong with me doing whatever I got to in order to get it."

"You really think you got the game all figured out. Sometimes you can't get everything you want, Deion."

"You already belong to me... you just don't

know it yet. I'll see you at seven. Bye, Diamond," Deion said, rubbing the puppy's head before getting in his car and driving off.

Chuck observed from a distance as Bernard, Lamont, and a few other workers patrolled the Santa Fe Villas. He knew they were trying to figure out the breakdown of how the operation was being run there, but based on the frustration on their faces, he knew they weren't having much luck. From what Chuck could see, it appeared they were arguing with each other. As he was taking some pictures, he noticed that Clip was calling.

"What up, boss?"

"How things going?"

"Well, I'm parked in front of Santa Fe now."

"Any movement?"

"Lots and none of it is in the other team's favor. From where I'm sittin' them dudes is takin' an 'L'. But I'm taking pictures so you can see for yourself."

"That's the sorta news I need. I allowed Alex

and Deion to take over all of our other territories but their determination to run Santa Fe Villas will be their downfall."

"You called it, boss, and everything is coming together exactly the way you said it would. You should feel good."

"I won't feel good until I destroy and dismantle Alex, Deion, and their entire crew. Them niggas gon' pay and they won't even see it coming."

Alex stood in the center of the empty 7,500 sq. ft. home he had purchased for him and Dahlia months ago. Due to the pain of losing her, he had never moved in, but at the same time his love for her wouldn't let him sell the house, until now. He decided to put the property on the market because for the first time since his fiancé's death, he knew it was time to move on. Holding on to the house they were supposed to share together as a family was his way of not letting go. But in order for his heart to begin the healing process, Alex could no longer hold onto the past, instead he had to embrace the present.

"You must be Alex Mills," he heard a woman say, shaking him out of his thoughts.

"Yes, and you are?"

"Anya." She smiled, reaching out her hand.

"Nice to meet you, Anya," Alex said, shaking her hand. "I don't mean to be rude, but what are you doing in my house?"

"Danny Sullivan sent me. I'll be handling the sale of your house."

"You're a realtor?"

"Yes.

"My apologies."

"No need to apologize. I should've made that known when I first walked in. But now that we've formally introduced ourselves, let's get down to business."

"Of course."

"Let me start off by saying, you have a beautiful home and a great location. You made a wise decision purchasing this property. Although you've had it less than a year, I believe we can sell it for a profit."

"Really? I'm surprised to hear that given

the market. I know the economy has supposedly stabilized and property values are supposed to be on the rise. But I still didn't think it had reached the climate where a profit would be possible."

"Impressive, I see you're well informed and for the most part you are correct. But this home is located in a highly coveted neighborhood with an excellent school system so you're in a winning situation. Areas like this are always the least affected when the market goes south."

"I guess I should thank Danny then. I originally wanted another house on the other side of town, but he insisted I get this one."

"Well, we both know Danny is a very smart man and you're smart too because you listened."

"Thank you."

"You're very welcome. Now, will you excuse me while I go take a look around and take some pictures so we can get this bad boy sold."

"By all means." Alex grinned. *Beauty, brains, and an engaging personality, this house will be sold before it hits the market,* Alex thought to himself admiring his new realtor.

Chapter 15
UNDENIABLE

"You look absolutely beautiful," Deion said, when he opened the car door for Calleigh. She was wearing a Givenchy black leather ruffled skirt with a fitted V-neck top and Tom Ford sandals. Her hair was slicked back in a side ponytail that draped over her shoulder. She finished off her polished, sexy look with a vivid lavender RiRi Boy Mac lipstick.

"Thank you. You look pretty handsome yourself." Deion had on a Lanvin midnight blue shawl collar blazer, a white tee that highlighted his jet black and icy white diamond prong setting chain, jeans, and a pair of navy Louboutin lace up shoes. The ensemble was classy yet hood street flashy, which summarized Deion's fashion style.

"This is a nice restaurant, I've never been here before," Calleigh commented, looking around Park 75 located inside the Four Seasons Hotel.

"I'm glad to be the first man to take you here and I'll be the last."

"Excuse me." Calleigh giggled nervously. "Did I hear you correctly?"

"Yes. I want you to be mine. I thought I already made that clear."

"Why is that?"

"Why do I want you to be mine?"

"Yes."

"Because you're exactly my type."

"And what type is that? Because from what I heard, you prefer strippers and partying and I'm neither of those."

"I make no apologies. I do enjoy strippers and women I can have fun with, but that's all it is, fun."

"So you don't want to have fun with me?"

"I do, but I want more than just that."

"You still haven't answered why?"

"Honestly, I'm not sure myself. All I know is, when I first saw you come into the lounge I was drawn to you. I loved your style. Even tonight, you look so well put together, sexy but classy. Then when I spoke to you, you were very articulate. I'm a street nigga to the core but I want my woman to exude some sophistication and you do that."

"Thank you, that's sweet of you to say."

"Just telling the truth. You make me wanna shower you wit' bags, shoes, and expensive shit. I like that." They both laughed. "But I've revealed a little bit about myself, now I wanna know more about you. How long you been in the A?"

"Not long, just a few months."

"What brings you here?"

"New York is great, but I needed a change. I was in grad school, but I wasn't focusing. I had some friends here and I thought maybe being in a new city would be good for me."

"Let me ask you something."

"Sure."

"I guess you can call me somewhat of a label

whore."

"What! What does that mean?"

"You know, designers and shit. I'm a street dude, but I love fashion. So the first night I met you, you were wearing a Roberto Cavalli dress, and tonight you have on Givenchy. How can you afford that and you a grad student?"

"I can't," Calleigh acknowledged. "I guess my ex-boyfriend was a label whore like you." She laughed. "That was one of his favorite things to do, take me shopping. So I might look like I have it like that, but I don't."

"This ex-boyfriend, is he the reason you left New York?"

"Yes. We went through a difficult breakup."

"Do you still have feelings for him? Is he my competition?'

"No, he is not your competition. That relationship is over with. He's my past and I have no desire to be with him ever again."

"I'm glad to hear that, so no need for us to mention him ever again. Let's talk about us. What time do you want me to pick you up tomorrow for our next date?"

"Can we get through this date first?"

"Are you tryna tell me that you not feeling me?" Calleigh put her head down for a moment to think before she answered the question. "Answer truthfully," Deion added.

"Okay fine. I'll admit that I was hoping you would say or do something to completely turn me off but..."

"But... continue."

"But, you've done just the opposite. You're winning me over just like you said you would."

"That's nothing to frown about," Deion said, reaching over the table and placing his hand on top of Calleigh's.

"I know you're a player, Deion. I just don't want you playing me."

"I won't. I promise."

"Don't make promises to me that you can't keep."

"Never that. Now look over your menu so we can order dinner. I know the waitress is tired of me putting my hand up, letting her know we're not ready."

"I'm sure she is."

"But before that, let's get a bottle of champagne. I believe we're gonna have a lot to celebrate."

"For some reason, Deion, I believe you're right."

"Of course. I'm always right," he said, giving a devilish grin.

While Calleigh looked over her menu, Deion couldn't take his eyes away from her. He couldn't believe his luck in finding his ideal woman right here in Atlanta. The crazy part is that Deion wasn't even looking to find another partner in life. As far as he was concerned, Alex was the only partner he needed, but meeting Calleigh had made him change his mind. If his gut feeling was correct, then Deion believed he had found the woman he would keep right by his side.

"I wanted to thank you for referring me to Anya," Alex said as he sat in Danny Sullivan's office. "She is an excellent realtor and I believe she'll have my home sold for a profit."

"I know she will, that's why I put her on it. Anya has done a lot of work for me and I haven't been disappointed yet. She always supersedes my expectations."

"So you've known her for awhile?" Alex inquired.

"Yes, a very long time."

"What can you tell me about her?"

"Why do I have the feeling that question has nothing to do with business."

"Is it that obvious?"

"I know you very well too, Alex, and I don't miss nothing."

"So does Anya have a man? Is she involved with anybody?"

"Not that I know of, but the only way you're going to find out for sure is if you ask her."

"True, but I didn't want to cross the line if she was already taken."

"All I can say is that Anya is a very smart, lovely woman and any man would be lucky to have her."

"As always, I appreciate your input."

"Of course you do. You know I'm a wise old man," Danny boasted with a smile. "I know business seems to be going very well for you but how's everything else?"

"You're referring to Dahila?"

Danny nodded his head yes. "I'm glad you're trying to get back out there on the dating scene."

"I wouldn't actually say that. I've been putting all my energy into work so I haven't had time or the desire to date. But since I started spending a significant amount of time with Anya, preparing to get my house on the market, I'm finding myself enjoying her company."

"That's a good thing. Listen, I know you suffered a terrible loss but you can't mourn forever and I bet your now-deceased fiancé wouldn't want you to. I don't know what will happen between you and Anya, but I think it's worth giving it a try."

"Yeah, you are a smart old man." Alex laughed. "I think I've taken up enough of your time. Plus, I got a phone call to make."

"That's my boy," Danny said, giving Alex thumbs up. "I'll talk to you later and good luck."

Danny winked his left eye.

As Alex was walking out the door he was dialing Anya's number. "Alex, hey how are you?"

"I'm good. How are you?"

"Great, is everything okay? Is there a problem with the house?"

"No, nothing like that. This phone call actually has nothing to do with business."

"Oh, then what is it?"

"I hope I'm not being too forward and if you feel I'm crossing the line, please, let me know because I wouldn't want anything to affect our business relationship."

"I'm lost. What are you talking about?"

"I wanted to invite you out for dinner."

"You mean like a date?"

"Yes, a date."

"Really, I mean—"

"I apologize, you're in a relationship with someone," Alex said, cutting Anya off. "Forget I asked.

"No... no... no. That's not it at all. I just had no idea you were interested in me. Alex, I would love to go out to dinner with you."

"Really?" A sigh of relief came over Alex. He hadn't asked a woman out for dinner in what seemed like forever and he couldn't believe how nervous he felt doing it.

"Yes," Anya confirmed again. Alex could sense her bright, cheerful smile coming through the phone, which only confirmed to him that he had made the right decision asking her out.

"Wonderful, how does tomorrow around six or seven work for you?"

"Eight would be perfect. I have to show a couple of houses late tomorrow to some potential buyers."

"Then I'll pick you up at eight."

"Great, I'll see you then. Bye." When Alex got off the phone with Anya the biggest smile crossed his face. A sense of enthusiasm from being around a woman he genuinely liked had been lacking for so long; Alex welcomed having that feeling back.

For the next few weeks it seemed Alex and Deion

were both enjoying the same thing—the company of being with a woman. Besides Passion, Deion had cut all other women out of his life. He was completely satisfied being with Calleigh and it had nothing to do with being intimate because they still hadn't had sex. Because of that, they spent most of their time getting to know each other.

"You wanna take a trip wit' me?" Deion asked, on their way to the movie theater.

"What kinda trip?"

"I was thinking maybe Hawaii."

"You want me to go to Hawaii with you?"

"Yeah, why not."

"You know how long that flight is?"

"Nope. I've never been."

"Me neither, but I heard the flight is ridiculous."

"Me, too. But I was told if you stop in LA first for a couple of days and then take your flight to Hawaii, it's not so bad. So what do you say?"

"I say let's do it."

"Great," Deion said, taking Calleigh's hand and kissing it. "Let's leave tomorrow."

"Tomorrow it is."

Chapter 16
LIVE YOUR LIFE

"Girl, it's been too long since we've hung out. I'm glad you were able to meet me for lunch," Shana said when she sat down with Passion at Twist restaurant in Phipps Plaza.

"Me, too. I've turned into a soccer mom since leaving the strip club."

"Well it seems to be working for you because you look great. Very well-rested and healthy, like you're taking care of yourself."

"I'm trying, but I do miss hanging out with you ladies at the club sometimes. We had a lot of fun there."

"Yeah, but you ain't missing nothing. We all

tryna get where you at. Off the pole with an excellent sponsor, who can financially take care of our needs. So you've hit the jackpot with Deion. Who would've thought somebody could tame Deion's ass. Well, not tame, but you know what I mean."

"No, I don't know what you mean, Shana."

"I mean Deion ain't gon' never be no one-woman man, but you know. But I'm sure you don't care. You living in the big house, don't have to work. Got all your bills paid. So what if he fucks around," Shana popped, sipping on her martini.

"What do you mean... you heard Deion was fucking around? Is it one of the girls at the strip club?"

"Nah, he hasn't been hanging out at the strip club for a while. But Kecia that work at that club said she saw him in the Gucci store with some chick. But who cares, you straight."

"I care," Passion said, getting choked up.

"Girl, I didn't mean to upset you. We both been in this game, we know how it works but you on the winning side right now."

"How am I winning Shana when he's out in

the Gucci store with some other woman? That's not winning to me."

"Oh fuck, you like really in love wit' that nigga."

"Yes, I'm in love with him. He ain't some guy in the club I'm dancing for to get tips."

"I mean, come on, Passion, that is how you met him."

"True. It might've started that way but that's not supposed to be our ending. Do you know the woman's name he was at the Gucci store with?"

"No, Kecia said she had never seen the chick before. But Passion, it's probably nothing. Just some flavor of the week Deion was trickin' on."

Passion didn't want Deion fuckin' around with anybody else, period. But if so, she did hope Shana was right, that the girl was just some flavor of the week. Unfortunately, Passion's instincts were telling her that wasn't the case at all. For a while now she felt things were changing between her and Deion, but the last few weeks something had been really off. He had been spending less and less time at her house and when he did come over it was really to just check up on Demonte. Passion tried to tell herself that Deion was simply busy running the streets due to work, but she could no longer lie to herself.

"Good afternoon, gorgeous," Alex said to Anya when she answered the phone.

"I got your flowers; they were waiting for me when I got to work. They're beautiful."

"Beautiful flowers for a beautiful woman. You've made these last few weeks incredible for me and it was my way of letting you know that."

"They've been amazing for me, too. I hope we're still on for tonight because I have a surprise for you. Alex, are you there?"

"I apologize, Anya," he said, looking down at his cell. Bernard was calling him back to back and now he had just sent a 911 text. "What did you say?"

"I said I hope we're still on for tonight because I have a surprise for you."

"We're definitely still on and I'll call you when I'm on the way. See you tonight," Alex said, rushing off the phone. When he hung up his landline he hit

Bernard back on his cell. "What's going on?"

"We had an issue over at Santa Fe Villas," Bernard said, clearly upset.

"I'm on the way," Alex said, grabbing his car keys before leaving his crib.

When Alex arrived at Santa Fe Villas he noticed Bernard and two other of his workers coming down a flight of stairs off to the side. The men were so caught up in their conversation that at first they didn't see Alex. It wasn't until he crossed the street and reached the sidewalk that they realized he was there.

"Yo, what's the emergency?" Alex questioned once his workers were standing in front of him.

"The unit we running our drugs out of."

"What about it?"

"Somebody ran up in it, killed Pete, and took the product."

"When did this happen?"

"Had to be in the last couple of hours because Lamont was there with him. Then I had Lamont bring me some heroin to the Washington Street Apartments. Once our other workers got to that location we came over here and found Pete."

"He still up there now?"

"Yeah, we didn't want to touch nothing until you gave the go 'head."

"Do you think it could've been a junkie that robbed him?"

"That's always a possibility, but most of the users over here ain't on no violent type shit."

"Let me go check things out," Alex said, heading towards the stairs with his men close behind him. When they reached the bottom stair, they all stopped in their tracks when a bullet came crashing through a front window, slightly grazing Lamont's shoulder. "Everybody get down!" Alex yelled as the men pulled out their guns.

Within a few seconds three men came running from behind some trees. Alex fired off a couple of shots before darting up the stairs. They weren't close enough to their cars so their next best option was to seek shelter in the apartment unit. The gunmen were quickly approaching, firing wildly in their direction.

Once they got to the apartment and before they could even lock the door, there was a loud Pop! Pop! Pop! causing Bernard to jump back as a bullet almost struck his hand. Alex motioned his hand for the three to split up as he went into a bedroom, Bernard slid into the bathroom, and Lamont hid in the other bedroom.

Alex could hear heavy breathing as a couple of the men headed towards the back room while another one stayed towards the front. One of the gunmen pushed the bedroom door open sticking his gun out, but the back of his head was facing Alex who was in the closet. Alex eased the door open pointing the gun to the back of the gunman's head and pulled the trigger. Pop! Pop! Pop!

All three bullets hit him in his head causing his body to fall face-first onto the bedroom floor. The second gunmen saw what had happened and leaped towards the bedroom to get at Alex, but Bernard caught him in the hallway, firing a bullet in his neck and back, killing him almost instantly as he bled out.

Before Bernard could get out of harm's way,

a bullet pierced through his upper thigh from the last gunman who was lurking in the front. Bernard managed to find haven back in the bathroom before another bullet hit him. Lamont busted off a few shots but the bullet graze from his shoulder had his aim off.

With the commotion going on in the hallway, Alex used the opportunity to storm out the bedroom, catching the third gunman off guard and emptying the last of his magazine on his upper torso. The powerful shots caused him to fall back, landing right on top of Pete's dead body as blood oozed out, saturating the beige carpet.

"Is everybody a'right?" Alex yelled out. Both Lamont and Bernard stepped out of their respective hiding positions nodding their heads yes. Each had injuries, but they were minor compared to the three dead men surrounding them, so they had no complaints.

After Passion finished having lunch with Shana, the

first thing she did when she got in her car was call Deion. Of course he wasn't answering his phone. Deion told her that he would be out of town for a week or so handling business, but she no longer believed that to be the truth. She began wondering if Deion had even left Atlanta and only told her that so she wouldn't bother him while he spent time with his new lady friend. After stopping by his apartment and a couple of other places, and coming up short, Passion decided to head to the lounge. The parking lot was pretty much empty except for a couple of cars. She noticed Reggie's Escalade in the front so she went to pick his brain. The front door was locked so Passion knocked on the glass.

"Passion, hey. We're not open yet," Reggie said, letting her come in.

"Oh, I'm sorry. I was just trying to get in touch with Deion, but he's not answering his phone. I know he's out of town, but I wanted to make sure he's alright."

"I'm sure he's fine. He's probably just busy. When he gets a moment I know he'll call you."

"You're right." Passion smiled sweetly. "Do you

have any idea when he'll be back from Houston?"

"Not sure. I know he's handling a lot of business in Houston for the rest of the week, so again, I'm not really sure."

"Okay, well if you speak to Deion before I do, please tell him to call me."

"Will do."

"Thanks."

"No problem... good seeing you, Passion."

"It's good to see you, too."

Reggie closed the door, locked it, and then immediately called Deion.

"Hey man, what's up?"

"Passion just left here."

"Is she okay? There's nothing wrong with Demonte is there?"

"Nah, nothing like that. She said she'd been calling you, but you haven't been answering so she was concerned."

"And what did you tell her?"

"That you were busy working. Handling business in Houston and..."

"Houston?" Deion asked, cutting Reggie off.

"Where you get Houston from?"

"Passion asked me did I know how long you would be in Houston so I assumed that's where you told her you was."

"Hell no! I told her I was in Maryland."

"Oh shit, my fault man."

"You didn't know Passion was gonna go completely Sherlock Holmes on you. I'll deal wit' her when I get back."

"A'ight, man, I'll see you in a few days."

"Bet."

"Is everything okay?" Calleigh asked when Deion got off the phone with Reggie.

"Everything's fine."

"Are you sure? You sounded a little upset," Calleigh said, sitting down on the bamboo canopy bed.

"How can I be upset when I'm at this crazy sexy island with you. I mean our hotel room is sitting on top of a cliff with views of Molokai Island. There's a tiered swimming pool connected by waterfalls and let's not forget about our private outdoor shower. Man, this place is so fuckin' beautiful I'm tempted to move here."

"It is breathtaking. I've never been anywhere this beautiful before," Calleigh said, staring out of the huge glass window that stretched across one full wall.

"It is, but it isn't as breathtaking as you," Deion said, lifting up Calleigh's hair and kissing her neck. Deion felt her body tense up so he stopped. "Are you afraid to be intimate with me?" he asked. They'd never had sex, but Deion thought being in a romantic place like Hawaii would put anyone in the mood, including Calleigh, to make love.

"No, of course I'm not afraid."

"Then what is it? We've known each other for a while now and we've never had sex. I didn't want to put any pressure on you, but I thought by now and being here, you would be ready."

"To be honest with you, I haven't been intimate with anyone since my ex and that was months ago. I'm just a little nervous, but I'm ready," Calleigh said, kissing Deion. He kissed her back before slipping off her white, silk and lace slip. Deion laid her back on the bed and admired her naked body for a moment.

"What's wrong?" Calleigh questioned.

"Absolutely nothing. You just so fuckin' beautiful I wanted to look at you. I'm a lucky man." Deion grabbed Calleigh by the waist and lifted her up to place her in the center of the bed. He lifted her leg, sprinkling kisses from the back of her ankle, down to the back of her thigh until he reached her wet insides. He licked Calleigh's clit and tongue fucked her pussy until her body couldn't take it anymore. Within seconds he made her cum, leaving her body shaking.

Deion grabbed her thighs and pulled Calleigh's body down to him. Before she had even finished her orgasm, Deion slid his dick in her dripping wet pussy, causing Calleigh to arch her back as he filled up her insides.

"Hmmmmm," Calleigh moaned as the initial pain of Deion's massive tool entering her turned into pleasure. Deion gently slid in and out, as he licked and bit on Calleigh's hardened nipples sending her body into another orgasm. Deion felt himself getting lost in her sweet juices and decided at that moment, Calleigh was the woman for him and he'd never let her go.

By the time Alex had finally arrived back home, he totally forgot about his date with Anya, until he realized she was blowing up his phone.

"Hello."

"What happened... where are you?"

"I'm sorry, Anya. I totally forgot about our date tonight."

"You forgot?" she asked, sounding offended.

"Yes. I had some problems with work and I'm just getting home. Again, I'm sorry but I'ma need to call you back," Alex said, abruptly hanging up the phone. He took off his clothes and headed straight to the shower. As the hot water drenched his body, Alex tried to figure out what the fuck happened today. His nerves were shot and stress level was rising at the thought that his organization might have to embark on a drug war.

When Alex got out of the shower he saw that he had a few missed calls from Anya and now she was calling back again. He tossed his phone down, not in the mood to talk to her or anybody else. The only person Alex did want to speak to was Deion, but he knew he was in Hawaii and didn't want to ruin his vacation. Especially since in all the years he'd known Deion, he had never gone on one. There was nothing he could do from Hawaii anyway, so Alex decided to wait until he got back to strategize what their next move should be.

Chapter 17
THE MESSAGE

Alex found himself swimming all up in Isabella although he was trying to leave her alone on the sex tip. But pounding his body inside of hers had become the perfect stress reliever for Alex. He had cum so hard that Alex almost fell asleep when he was done.

"You felt incredible," Isabella whispered, wishing Alex could live inside of her forever. "You're my best addiction."

"Isabella, I have a lot on my mind. I'm not in the mood to talk."

"Okay, then don't talk, just listen. Whatever you need I'm here for you; whether it be pleasuring you sexually, or if you need some assistance handling business. All you have to do is ask. I'm going to take a shower, but please stay as long as you want." Isabella kissed him on the lips then went to the bathroom. Alex closed his eyes and fell into a deep sleep.

"Boss, we had a setback," Chuck told Clip when he arrived at the house he was staying at.

"What sort of setback?"

"Three of our men got killed over at Santa Fe Villas when they tried to ambush some workers of Alex and Deion's crew," Chuck explained, not knowing that one of the men had been Alex himself. "They did manage to kill one of his men and take some product from the unit they're using to sell drugs."

"Fuck! We supposed to be eliminating men not losing some of our own," Clip barked.

"I know. No doubt things didn't go the way we planned but I'm sure we've shut down their operations over at Santa Fe for the time being."

"I don't know, Chuck. Alex and Deion are going to react in one of two ways. Shut down shop at Santa Fe or come harder, killing everything moving over there. Only time will tell, but we should know very shortly."

"So what do you want me to do?"

"Just wait. Don't have any of our men make a move until we have an idea what they're going to do first because we can't afford to lose any more workers. We've lost more than enough already."

"Understood."

Clip was furious about what happened at the Santa Fe Villas, but wasn't discouraged. He had a back up plan in effect to guarantee that Alex and Deion would go down for good.

Passion sat at her kitchen table ready to stand up and break every glass, plate, bowl, anything that she could shatter in a thousand pieces. Instead she remained motionless. Her heart was aching. After her conversation with Reggie, there left no doubt that Deion had gone out of town with a woman. More than likely the female he had been seen at the Gucci store with. Passion didn't understand how the script had flipped on her so quickly and how she should proceed. Deion still hadn't returned any of her phone calls only sending a text asking how she and Demonte were doing. As question after question flipped around in Passion's head, she noticed Shana was calling.

"Hey, what's up?"

"You busy... you got a minute to talk?"

"Yeah, I can talk. What's going on?"

"I know during our last conversation you asked me if I knew who the girl was at the Gucci store with Deion."

"You found out her name?" Passion questioned, becoming anxious.

"I'm not sure if this is the same chick, but I think most likely it is."

"Okay, Shana, just tell me."

"This girl name Dominique is cool with one of the dancers at the club. She came in last night with some friends and you know girls get to running off at the mouth and she mentioned that her friend Calleigh was in Hawaii with Deion."

Her world seemed like it stopped, coming to a complete halt for Passion. She couldn't feel her heart beating and she could've sworn she no longer had a pulse.

"Passion, are you there?" Shana yelled out, reminding her that even though it felt like death, she wasn't dead.

"Yes, I'm here," Passion replied in an almost inaudible tone. "Did this girl say anything else?"

"Just that they had been dating for awhile and the relationship was serious."

"Is the girl from here?"

"She lives here now in that subdivision Buckhead Place Townhouses, but she moved here from New York."

"I see."

"I hate bringing you bad news, but I knew you would want to know."

"Do you know when they're supposed to be coming back?"

"Tomorrow."

"Thanks, Shana."

"No problem. You know I got you, girl," Shana said, before hanging up the phone.

The information that Shana just delivered did make Passion get up out her chair and open up the kitchen cabinet and start throwing shit. Luckily her son Demonte was at her mother's house for the weekend because it sounded like explosions were going off as Passion threw every piece of glass she could get her hands on. One after another, the dishes went crashing to the floor. The tears streaming down her face made what Passion was doing a blur. She didn't stop until a piece of glass cut her finger and she tasted the dripping blood.

"Do you know what time Deion's flight gets in today?" Alex asked Reggie.

"We spoke right before he was boarding his flight and I think he said six," Reggie answered, going over some invoices.

"You didn't mention the shootout?" Alex

wanted to know.

"Nah, you said not to," Reggie responded, glancing up for second.

"Good. I'm glad he's coming back today because I need to speak to him and get his input on what we should do."

"He said after he dropped Calleigh off at home he would swing by here."

"Deion and this Calleigh chick are gettin' pretty serious, huh?" Alex probed.

"It seems that way. Honestly, I ain't never seen him this open over a chick before," Reggie said, with a slight laugh.

"That's what I was thinking and he took her on vacation. Deion is a workaholic, he never goes on vacation. Have you met this woman yet?" Alex was curious to know.

"No, but I saw her the night Deion met her for the first time. I can't lie, she is beautiful and Deion said she's equally as sweet." Reggie smiled.

"Sweet and beautiful, what the hell is she doing with Deion?" They both laughed. "I'm happy for him though. Deion is the last person I ever thought would have a serious relationship with a woman."

"I agree. But he's been taken with Calleigh from the first moment he saw her walk through those double doors," Reggie said, pointing towards the entrance. "I just wonder how his relationship with Passion is gonna play out. I don't think either of those women will be interested in a love triangle. Speaking of triangles, what's up with you and Isabella? Has her husband gotten hip to what ya got going on yet?"

"Reggie, I was doing good. I had met someone that I really liked. I wasn't thinkin' 'bout Isabella. But then..."

"Then what?"

"Then that shit happened at Santa Fe and I had all this frustration I needed to release. Isabella was what I needed."

"That's what they got gyms for and boxing classes, to release frustration. That stress reliever sex never ends well."

"Yeah, yeah, but it damn sure feels good."

Passion had been waiting at the entrance of the Buckhead Place Townhomes laying in wait for Deion and Calleigh all day. She had no idea what time their flight was getting in, all she knew was that they arrived some time today. Passion also wasn't sure which townhouse Calleigh lived in, so it made sense to her to find a discreet parking space that gave her a clear view of all the cars coming in and out of the subdivision.

Passion glanced down at her watch and saw it was a quarter to seven. "Where the hell are they? Maybe they're on one of those flights that don't get in until after midnight. It doesn't matter because I'm not leaving," Passion said, talking to herself out loud. For a brief second, Passion yawned, closing her eyes, and when she opened them, she caught Deion driving through the entrance in his silver Aston Martin. Passion recognized that car anywhere because of the specialty rims Deion had made for it. She watched, but waited for a few moments for

Deion to drive past her before starting her car and trailing them from a safe distance. He ended up making the second right before pulling up in the driveway on the left-hand side.

Passion kept driving to the end of the cul-de-sac and turned around, parking off to the side out of their view. She saw Deion and then Calleigh get out the car. Deion popped the trunk retrieving three pieces of luggage and taking them inside. He appeared to be in a rush because once he brought the luggage inside he came right back out. Passion saw Calleigh follow him and then they gave each other a long lingering kiss. Passion rolled down her window trying to see if she could hear anything they were saying to each other, but she was parked too far away. After kissing one last time, Deion got back in his car and drove away.

After a couple of minutes, Passion got out of her car and sprinted to Calleigh's front door. She rang the doorbell and in a matter of seconds she could hear her unlocking the door.

"Did you come back to give me another kiss." Calleigh opened the door smiling. "I'm sorry,

I thought you were my boyfriend. How can I help you?"

"What do I need to do so you can stop fuckin' wit' my man?" Passion stood with her arms folded, waiting to hear Calleigh's response.

"I think you're knocking on the wrong door because I don't know you or your man. Now, excuse me," Calleigh said, about to close the door, but Passion pushed it back open.

"You do know my man! His name is Deion and he just dropped you off!" Passion screamed, forcing her way inside Calleigh's home.

"I'ma need you to get out of my house!" Calleigh screamed back.

"I'm not going anywhere until you answer my question. What do I need to do so you can stop fuckin' wit' my man?"

"So wait, Deion is your man, but I was in Hawaii with him for a week. Something about that equation ain't adding up. You sounding like a bitter ex to me."

"To be an ex, two people have to break up which hasn't happened. Deion and I are very much together. I'm still living in that big ass house he bought for my son and me."

"You all have a son together?"

"No, he's my son, but Deion takes care of him like he's his very own. Demonte thinks of him as a father. We're a family and I don't want you or anybody else fuckin' that up."

"You come to my crib, disrespecting me, what the fuck do you want me to do!"

"I want you to leave Deion alone. I'm asking you, woman to woman," Passion said, humbling herself. "You have no idea what I've been through wit' Deion. I can't let him go. I won't let him go." Passion now had tears in her eyes as she tried to get through to Calleigh.

"I need you to go," Calleigh said, putting her hand on the door.

"I'll leave and I know you don't owe me shit, but Deion isn't some trick for me. He saved my life in more ways than you can ever understand. Our relationship is complicated. I know you haven't been seeing him that long so you can still walk away... no foul no harm. There are plenty of other men out there. But besides my son, Deion is my life. So please, just think about that," Passion begged, then walked out the door.

"I done came back home to some straight bullshit," Deion spit as he, Alex, and Reggie sat at the bar stumped. "I mean ain't no major crews left out here. Everybody basically come to us for their product in these parts. So I'm tryna figure out who would even have enough balls to start a war wit' us."

"We've been tryna figure out the same thing. We got Bernard out there questioning these low on the totem pole type dudes seeing what the streets is sayin'." Alex huffed, balling up his napkin. "So far no luck. The real question is, what should be our next move? Do we need to shut down shop at Santa Fe Villas? 'Cause of my own personal vendetta I was the one that pushed for that location, but we've already lost one worker, I don't want to lose any more."

"Fuck that, we can't back down now. We'll look like some sucker ass niggas and we can't go out like that," Deion said, shaking his head. "If need be, we'll send a message. Motherfuckers wanna start it, but we gon' end it. Let's put our men back on location, but this time triple up. Anybody glance at one of them niggas wrong they gotta just kill 'em."

"I agree," Reggie chimed in. "With GMC gone, you and Alex have these streets on lock. Ya known as the niggas that got all the power. If motherfuckers think ya weak then they'll be ready to taste blood... ya's blood."

"So you in, Alex?" Deion asked, turning to his partner.

"I was hoping we wouldn't have to get involved in a street war, but we gotta protect what we built. So yeah, I'm in."

"I'll gather all the men and decide which ones to put at the Santa Fe location," Reggie said as he and Alex went back and forth discussing the different workers. Deion should've been a part of the conversation, but he had become preoccupied reading the text messages from Calleigh flooding his phone.

"Yo, I have to go handle something. I'll call ya

later on."

"Man, you just got back in town. Where you runnin' off to now?" Reggie wanted to know.

"I have a situation wit' Calleigh I need to deal wit'."

"We dealin' wit' important business and you runnin' off for a chick?" Reggie questioned, in disbelief.

"First off, Calleigh ain't some chick, she's my woman. Now, in regards to business, I already explained how that shit needs to be handled. I'll be at the warehouse first thing tomorrow to make sure the workers that's gonna be assigned to Santa Fe know what to do. Now, I gotta go."

"That nigga got it bad," Reggie said, walking over to the door and locking it after Deion left.

"You ain't lyin'. I'm not used to seeing Deion like this. I don't know how to take it, but we can't worry about that man's personal life right now," Alex said. "We gotta get ourselves prepared in case whoever orchestrated that ambush decides to try again."

"Calleigh, open the door," Deion barked, after he had been knocking for a few minutes. "I'm not leaving until you open the fuckin' door!"

A couple of more minutes passed until finally, Calleigh let Deion in. "I'm not doing this with you, Deion. You lied to me."

"Just let me explain."

"You mean let you lie to me some more."

"That's not what I'm tryna do," he said, caressing the side of Calleigh's face.

"Don't touch me," she said, moving away.

"I can always touch you, you belong to me."

"Would that be the same way Passion belongs to you, too."

"My relationship with Passion is complicated."

"So you're admitting you're in a relationship with her?"

"Yes."

"You love her?"

"Yes, I have love for her, but it's not the same

kind of love I have for you."

"Is that supposed to make me feel better? You promised me that you would never play me and that's exactly what you've done."

"How have I played you?"

"You have a girlfriend, Deion. I would've never gotten involved with you if I knew you had somebody."

"Passion is not my girlfriend and the only person that has me is you."

"You just admitted you're in a relationship with her and that you love her."

"It's complicated."

"That's funny because Passion described you all's relationship the same way. Either you all are together or you're not together. You can't have it both ways, Deion."

"Like I said, you're my woman. I'm with you."

"Then leave her alone. Cut her out of your life!"

"I can't do that."

"Excuse me?"

"I can't cut Passion out my life. She and her

son are like family to me, but that doesn't affect what we have and I'll make sure she knows not to ever bother you again. I promise baby," Deion said, leaning down to kiss Calleigh.

"Have you had sex with her since we've been seeing each other?" she questioned, stepping back.

"What?"

"Don't 'what' me. Answer the question. Have you been having sex with Passion since we started seeing each other?"

"A few times. But you and I weren't even having sex yet. Things are different now between us."

"So what, since we started having sex, you're going to now stop having sex with her! You are such a fuckin' liar. Get out! I'm done with you!"

"You don't mean that, Calleigh."

"Oh yes the fuck I do. Now get out because unlike Passion, you don't pay no bills here. Now get out!"

"If I didn't love you so much I would knock the shit outta you right now."

"You don't love me, now get out!" Calleigh screamed, rushing to the door and swinging it open.

Deion took his time walking to the door and stood by the entrance staring at Calleigh, but she refused to make eye contact with him. "I know you upset and I can't say that I blame you, but I'm not letting you go."

"You don't have a choice."

"That's where you're wrong," were Deion's departing words.

Chapter 18
Don't Be Afraid

"I want a divorce," Isabella said casually as she sat across from Joaquin having breakfast. Joaquin continued reading his newspaper as if he didn't hear a word Isabella had said. "Don't you have anything to say?"

"What do you want me to say, Isabella? You want a divorce. I'm not going to give you one. There's nothing left to discuss," he said, never taking his eyes off the article he was reading.

"Joaquin, this marriage has been over for years. You have a couple of mistresses and numerous girlfriends. You don't love me and I don't love you."

"Marriage isn't based on love, my darling. It's

a business arrangement and why would I mess up our arrangement when it's absolutely perfect."

"It might be perfect for you, but it's disgusting for me. I want to move on with my life and that doesn't include you, Joaquin. Because of me you've made more than enough business connections and will continue to do extremely well after our divorce."

"That might be true, but we both know the clout your family has in this business. I won't be able to command the same level of respect if we get a divorce."

"It's always about you, Joaquin, but that is no longer my problem."

"What has changed with you? Why are you so determined to get a divorce now? You've always known about my other women. That has never been a secret. So why, after all these years, have you decided that divorce is now the only option? Unless, you have found someone else," Joaquin said, tossing down his paper, burning a hole through Isabella with his stare.

"Jealousy isn't becoming of you, Joaquin."

"You listen to me, Isabella. You are my wife. You

will never disrespect me by being with another man. I won't allow it or tolerate it. Do you understand?"

"Joaquin, this marriage is over and we will get a divorce. It can end amicably or it can get hostile. The choice is yours. Now excuse me, I have work to do," Isabella said, getting up from the table, leaving Joaquin fuming.

"You haven't called me, returned my texts, or been here for two weeks. What type of shit is that, Deion?" Passion asked, sitting outside by the pool, getting energy from the sun.

"You know why I haven't been fuckin' wit' you for the last couple weeks, Passion."

"Because you was pissed that I went and checked that lil' side piece bitch you fuckin' wit'."

"You see this pool you lounging by. This big fuckin' house you living in, and that nice fuckin' car you drive, that's all my shit and I can take it back anytime I want. You want to keep all this shit, then stay in yo' fuckin' lane. Are we clear?"

"I don't care about none of this shit!" Passion cried out.

"Oh really? So you wanna take yo' ass back to that motherfuckin' strip pole and shake yo' tits and ass for dollas again. Go back to yo' struggle life then."

"Why would you do that to me? Why would you threaten to send me back there?"

"You doin' it to yo'self by gettin' involved in a situation that has nothing to do wit' you."

"That Calleigh bitch means that much to you? What makes her so special? Is it because you didn't find her in a strip club like you found me?"

"You and I both know this relationship would've been over wit' if it wasn't for Demonte and for me feeling guilty for what Terrance did to you."

"Why are you being so cruel to me, Deion, when all I've ever done was love you."

"I'm not being cruel to you, I'm being honest. Calleigh is my woman, but you and Demonte are family to me. I'll always take care of you as long as you stay in yo' lane. That lane means never ever steppin' to Calleigh again. Because if you do, all of this good living is gonna disappear like that," Deion said, snapping his finger.

"I'm not giving up on us, Deion. I love you like I love Demonte, unconditionally. She'll never give you that."

Deion stared at Passion who was lying back in her bikini. Her deep tanned skin was the perfect contrast against the curved back of the sailcloth shell colored, resin basket weave harbor chaise. Deion still found her to be a sexy woman and believed her when she said she loved him unconditionally. But whether he was with Calleigh or not, in Deion's mind she would never qualify to be his woman. Passion would always have to play the role of one of many. Deion believed if she could accept that position all would be lovely in their relationship. If she tried to fight against it, Deion knew he would have no choice but to cut Passion off for good.

"I was glad to hear from you. I thought things had ended between us," Anya said, sitting down on Alex's couch.

"I want to apologize for that, Anya. In my line of business, things can get very stressful. I've been dealing with a lot these last few weeks and I didn't want to burden you with my problems or have you deal with my bad mood."

"Alex, I'm a grown woman. I know in relationships things aren't always going to be perfect. I don't want you to shut me out because you don't think I'm cut out to deal with your problems and bad mood. Unless you asked me over here because you're not interested in us having that sort of relationship and you wanted to tell me that in person."

"Anya, that's not it at all. I haven't enjoyed being around a woman as much as you since Dahlia. You make me feel like I have a second chance at love. But I'll admit that also scares me."

"Why would that scare you?"

"Because I don't ever want to love someone that much again and lose them."

"I can understand you feeling that way. To lose your fiancé and unborn child would make any man reluctant to fall in love again. But I want you to give us a chance. It might not work, nothing is guaranteed, but I think you're worth the risk and I hope you think I am, too."

"I do think you're worth it," Alex said, before leaning in and kissing Anya. Her lips felt so soft against his. All Alex wanted to do was carry her to his bedroom so they could make love, but he fought the urge.

"I want to feel you inside of me," Anya whispered between their kisses.

"I wanna feel inside of you, too," Alex replied, as his dick got rock hard. It would've been so easy for Alex to undress Anya and explore every inch of her body, but he held back, mainly because of Isabella.

For the last few weeks, Alex and Isabella had been intimate on a pretty consistent basis. Even though it was mainly just sex for Alex he knew it meant a lot more to Isabella. Because they did do business together, he didn't want to hurt her. Alex also didn't want to hurt Anya. He didn't think it would be fair to be going back and forth having sex with both women. Until he ended the sexual part of his relationship with Isabella for good, Alex wanted to hold off starting one with Anya.

"Make love to me then," Anya said, unbuttoning his shirt.

"I want to so bad, but baby we need to wait." Alex moaned, still kissing Anya but stopping her from unbuttoning his shirt.

"Why... why do we have to wait?"

"Baby, just trust me. I want us to start things off right. Let me get my business under control so the only thing I'm thinking about is you. Okay?"

"Okay."

"Now give me another kiss before I get back to work."

"I could stay here and kiss you all day," Anya said, playfully biting down on Alex's bottom lip. "But I'm going to leave so you can get back to work."

"I'll call you later on. I'll take you to dinner."

"How about I cook you dinner instead."

"I would like that."

"Great, I'll see you later on." Anya smiled, then left. Alex was pleased that he reconnected with Anya. He felt there might be a real opportunity for them to build a future together, after all.

"I'm going to keep coming back here everyday until you talk to me," Deion yelled, as he stood in front of Calleigh's front door. "Please answer the door. I have something for you," Deion announced, hoping that would get her to let him in. "Don't make me beg, Calleigh."

Deion had not given up on getting Calleigh back since she threw him out of her townhouse. He knew she was upset, but he had no idea that two weeks later he would still be begging for her to give him another chance. At this point, he was becoming frustrated because normally, Calleigh would have said something to him, even if it was to just leave her alone. But today, she was completely ignoring him, which Deion hated.

Deion began wondering if Calleigh was home, but figured she had to be since her car was parked out front, that was until he saw a Maserati pulling up in Calleigh's driveway. Deion had parked across the street and because there was a tree that obscured her door entrance, at first Calleigh didn't notice Deion was waiting for her. But when she got out the car with some guy and Deion walked up on them, Calleigh was completely startled.

"Deion, I didn't realize you were here."

"I see. Who the fuck is he, Calleigh?" Deion snapped, pointing towards the man that had gotten out of the car.

"No need to get upset, we all grown here," the man responded.

"Yo nigga, shut tha fuck up! I wasn't talkin' to you," Deion popped, walking up on the man.

"Deion, stop! He works with me at my job. Something is wrong with my car so he gave me a ride home."

"If you need a ride home, you call me. You understand... and if you just droppin' her off, why the fuck you get out the car?" Deion questioned, placing his attention back on the man.

"I just needed to use the restroom, that's all."

"Nigga, please. Save that bullshit. Get yo' ass back in the motherfuckin' car and get outta here!"

"Is that what you want, Calleigh, for me to

leave?"

"What tha fuck did you just ask her?" Deion questioned.

"Man, I'm not talking to you. I'm speaking to Calleigh." Before the man could say another word, Deion lounged forward landing a powerful punch that sent the man hitting the cement face first.

"Deion, what have you done!" Calleigh screamed out, running over to her co-worker.

"Get the fuck in the house, right now!" Deion demanded, grabbing Calleigh's arm.

"Get off of me," she yelled, yanking her arm away. "Robert, are you okay?" Calleigh asked, trying to help him up.

"I'm fine. Calleigh you sure you don't want to leave with me. I don't think it's safe for you to stay here."

"You must be dying for me to put my foot up yo' ass, 'cause you still runnin' yo' fuckin' mouth," Deion barked, about to swing on the man again but Calleigh stepped in between the two.

"Robert, just get in your car and go, please." The man hesitated for a second. "Please, Robert, go…

now," Calleigh insisted. Robert finally took Calleigh's advice, got in his car, and drove off.

"Yo, what the fuck is wrong wit' you!" Deion screamed, grabbing Calleigh's arm again.

"What's wrong with me? What's wrong with you! You have no right to be here and question me. I'm not even with you anymore."

Deion gripped the bottom of Calleigh's chin and held it firmly. "You want me gone? You want me out yo' life? Huh? Answer me, is that what you want?" Calleigh nodded her head yes. "Fine, I'll leave. You win. I won't bother you ever again," Deion said, releasing her from his grasp.

Calleigh kept her head down not watching as Deion walked away. She heard the car door open, which made her turn around. "Don't go," Calleigh yelled out.

Deion was already sitting down in the car, but the door wasn't closed. "What did you say?" he asked, rising back up.

"I said, don't go."

"Which one is it, Calleigh? Do you want me to stay or leave?"

"I want you to stay," she said, going over to Deion.

"Why don't you just accept that you mine?" Deion said, lifting Calleigh's face up.

"I just want you to be mine, too."

"I am yours."

"Only mine and nobody else's. Do you want to have to share me with another man?"

"Don't ask me a question like that. You already know what would happen if I even thought you were with somebody else."

"Then how do you think I feel knowing you have somebody else?"

"I'm not with anybody else. I told you I would handle the situation with Passion and I did. You don't ever have to share me with anybody else. You understand?"

"Yes. I'm just so in love with you."

"I know you are, 'cause I'm in love with you, too. I've never told a woman that and I mean it. I've been miserable these last couple of weeks. I don't ever wanna be without you again."

"Me neither. Come on, let's go inside so you

can show me how much you've missed me."

"Before we do that, I have something for you. What do you think?"

"What do I think of what? Where is it?"

"This," Deion said, extending his hand out.

"This, car?"

"Yep. It's a brand new 2014 S550 Sedan, Diamond White Metallic. Go look inside. Nothing like that new car smell."

"I can't believe you got this for me."

"I brought it over here today to surprise you. For the last couple of weeks nothing I did or said would make you forgive me. When I got you this car, I said to myself, if I still don't get you back, I didn't know what I would have to buy you next."

"Baby, you're such a mess, but I guess you my mess," Calleigh said, giving Deion a kiss. "Now let's go inside before I can't resist you any longer and I start taking your clothes off right now."

"Lead the way or better yet, let me carry you." Deion smiled, lifting Calleigh up and carrying her inside.

Chapter 19
DEADLY CHOICES

Alex was on I-85 on his way to see Isabella. For the first time in weeks everything in his life seemed to be on an even keel. The drama at Santa Fe Villas had simmered down and it seemed to be under control. Initially, when their men set up shop again, a couple of local dealers tried to give them some problems, but like Deion predicted, once they were roughed up, the message spread quickly and people stopped fucking with them.

Not only was business good, but so was his personal life. The slow, but steady, approach was working well for his relationship with Anya. They were becoming closer and not only was he attracted to her physically but also mentally. The only issue that was stopping them from proceeding to the next level was his relationship with Isabella. He had ended things once before with her when he got serious with Dahlia, but after her death, Alex found himself going back to familiar territory. He didn't want to end things with Isabella again only to wind up back in bed with her. He wanted to move with caution so there would be no bad blood between anybody involved. As Alex debated the best way to handle Isabella, his thoughts came to a halt when he heard his phone ringing.

"Deion, what's up, man?"

"Not shit. Listen, I'ma need that hookup wit' Isabella. My connect talkin' crazy wit' them prices again so I wanna lock in this other shit so I can give that motherfucker the middle finger."

"No problem. What you doing now?"

"I have to make a stop at one of the warehouses, but after that I'm free. Why, what's up?"

"I'm actually on my way to meet with Isabella now. I was gonna say, if you can meet me over there and we can get that shit locked down today."

"Perfect. Let me take care of this shit at the warehouse and I'll come to you. She still be staying at the Four Seasons?"

"Nah, she got a townhouse over in East Chastain Park. I'll text you the exact address."

"Cool. I'll see you in a little bit."

"Deion and Alex have pretty much become untouchable at this point. Instead of bowing out when shit got hot they came harder so now the streets see them as unbeatable," Chuck informed Clip. Chuck dreaded making the long drive to the house on the outskirts of Atlanta to have this conversation with his boss, but he knew it needed to be done in person and not over the phone.

"I figured that would be the move they'd make, because I would've done the same," Clip said, stepping away from the table and walking over to the window.

"What do you want me to do next? I can round up some more men and we can get this poppin'. We gotta lot of soldiers out here ready to put in work. I think I should make some calls," Chuck suggested.

"You never start a war you know you can't win," Clip stated, calmly. "We don't have the manpower to beat them. That hit at Santa Fe Villas was to test the waters and we lost three men in the process. A wise man knows when it's time to cut his losses and let go."

"What are you saying, you want us to give up taking Deion and Alex down?"

"No, that's not what I said."

"Then what, 'cause them niggas gotta pay for what they did to Laron and the rest of the Get Money Crew," Chuck shouted, getting worked up. "Them motherfuckers can't get away with this shit."

"And they won't. I always have a backup plan and it's already in affect. Alex and Deion will go down. I put that on everything I love."

"Alex, you're the only man I know that always puts a smile on my face every time I see you," Isabella said, greeting him at the door.

"And you always know the right thing to say to stroke my ego," Alex said, placing a kiss on Isabella's cheek.

"That's the best I can get, a kiss on the cheek?" she asked, closing the door.

"We have a lot of business to discuss. I don't want us to get sidetracked. Also, my partner, Deion, is coming over. He wants to talk to you about your coke prices."

"You know I'll give you whatever you need and at the best prices, Alex. What time is your partner coming over?"

"He just sent me a text and said in about an hour," Alex said, sitting down on the couch. "By the way, your new place is beautiful and very spacious. What is this, almost 4,000 square feet?"

"Yes, almost. I like it too, very quiet. There are only 10 units in the building. You should look into buying one, then we would be neighbors." Isabella was now standing in front of Alex. She kneeled down and began taking off his belt.

"Isabella, what are you doing?"

"What does it look like I'm doing?"

"I told you we have business to discuss."

"Your partner won't be here for an hour. We can discuss your business and his business at the same time. That way we can have a little fun before he gets here." Her lips were so inviting that Alex couldn't resist. "Lets go upstairs. I want you to bless my bed." She licked her lips, taking Alex's hand and leading him upstairs.

By the time they got upstairs and reached the bedroom, Isabella was out of her wrap dress and Alex's clothes had left a trail leading to the bed. She was in the mood to be in control so Isabella straddled Alex as he gripped her ass, pushing his dick deeper inside of her. She rubbed her tits, moaning in pleasure, which turned him on even more.

As Alex stroked hard and deep, Isabella couldn't control her cries of pleasure and whimpering. The intensity of their lovemaking had them both unmindful to their surroundings. "Oh yes, baby, I love you baby," Isabella purred, as her wide hips rocked in rhythm to Alex's strokes.

"You disgusting whore!" Joaquin roared,

bringing to a complete stop the passionate sex session. Isabella turned around and locked eyes with her husband. His face would be the last she'd see before Joaquin sprayed her upper body with five bullets. Isabella's dead body slumped down on Alex as her blood drenched his chest.

"Isabella," he mumbled in a low voice. Alex was in shock that less than a minute ago he was having incredible sex with her and now Isabella was lying on top of him dead.

"You... you.... you cross me!" Joaquin yelled with spit flying out of his mouth.

"Joaquin, relax, calm down," Alex said, trying to talk him down.

"You tell me to relax and I catch you fuckin' my wife! You traitor! I help you! I make you a very rich man and this is how you show me gratitude," Joaquin continued yelling, aiming his gun at Alex's head. "You will join my whorish wife in hell!"

Alex closed his eyes as he heard the ringing of bullets in the air. He had no desire to look at Joaquin's face and witness his own death. Alex's life flashed him by and with all the ways he had imagined dying, in bed with a married woman was never a scenario. A few seconds later the ringing noise of bullets stopped. Alex was reluctant to open his eyes but he didn't feel the burning sensation of hot led ripping through his skin, so he realized he had to still be alive.

"Man, you a'ight? You bleeding?"

"Deion, I have never been so happy to see you in my fuckin' life."

"Is that yo' blood? Do you need to get to the hospital?"

"No, that's Isabella's blood," Alex said, solemnly.

"Do we need to take her to the hospital?"

"No, she's gone." Alex gently moved Isabella's dead body off his chest and covered her with the bedspread.

"Alex, man, when I walked in here I thought Joaquin had already killed both of ya."

"If you had gotten here any later, that's what would've happened."

"You go take a shower. I'ma call our clean up crew and get this shit taken care of."

"I can't believe Isabella is dead," Alex kept

saying over and over again. "If I had stopped fuckin' wit' her a long time ago she would still be alive."

"Man, you can't think about that shit no more. You fucked up, we all fuck up. It's in the past... we gotta move on. Now go get yo'self cleaned up so we can get outta here."

Deion glanced down at Joaquin and then at Isabella. "I guess I won't be gettin' them cheap ass coke prices after all," he smacked, shaking his head.

"Baby, where are you taking me?" Calleigh whined, ready to take off the blindfold."

"Calm yo' ass down, we're almost there," Deion said, getting off East Conway between Jett Road and Northside Drive. "And don't you dare take that shit off." They would've reached their destination a long time ago but Friday traffic in Atlanta was ridiculous so it was holding things up.

"I'm just anxious. You always have the best surprises." Calleigh smiled.

"Well this is the best surprise yet," Deion said.

"Now you can take it off."

Calleigh was speechless as they drove through the iron gates of the private Buckhead Estate. The European-designed home was nothing less than exquisite. "Deion, I know you're not thinking about buying this house," Calleigh said, as they got out of the car and walked inside.

"No, I'm not thinking about buying it, I already did. It's ours, that is, if you move in with me."

"Of course I'll move in with you," Calleigh screamed, giving Deion a hug. I can't believe I'm going to be living in this house." She beamed, looking around at the Italian Arch and beautiful custom details. The over 9,000 square-foot-home had too many features to name. But the 13' ceilings, outdoor living with loggia pool, and elevator were just a few of the extravagant details.

"Then welcome home, baby," Deion said, lifting Calleigh up and kissing her.

"Do you know how much I love you?" Calleigh said, wrapping her legs around his waist and her arms around his neck.

"Yes, and I love you just as much if not more,"

Deion said, as their kisses became longer and more fervent. "You belong to me. You're my world and I want to spend the rest of my life with you." Deion meant every word he said. He had never believed in terms like soulmate, or I found the woman I want to spend the rest of my life with. Those were things he never even thought about until meeting Calleigh. As crazy and irrational as Deion could be, she gave him the calmness he needed to balance himself out. He felt at ease to discuss who he was and the life he led without worrying that Calleigh would ever cross him or judge him for the decisions he makes. He trusted her with his heart, which made Deion love her that much more.

Chapter 20
LOVE, LIES, RESENTMENT

2 Months Later...

"This is nice. I'm enjoying dinner with my best friend, his woman, and the love of my life. It don't get no better than this. Let's make a toast," Deion said, as they all raised their glasses. "There's one life, one love, but we have two kings and now we have our queens. Cheers!"

"Cheers," they all said in unison, clicking their champagne glasses.

"So Alex, when you and Anya gon' move into a crib like this?" Deion said, putting him on the spot.

He wouldn't have done so if he didn't already know that his best friend was officially on serious status with Anya.

"Now that you mention it, we have been discussing getting a place together, but I doubt it will be something of this caliber. This is a little too excessive for my taste." Alex laughed.

"Yeah, Alex is more on the conservative side." Anya nudged his arm lovingly.

"True, Deion and I have always moved a tad differently in that area. He's the flashy, extravagant one. You don't half do shit. You gon' go hard or you ain't gon' go at all."

"You right about that," Deion agreed.

"That's Deion for you. He only likes the best. He had all our furniture custom-designed," Calleigh added. "He's so meticulous. He doesn't even let me pick out my own clothes. He has a personal shopper that gets everything for me."

"I only want the best for you," he said, kissing Calleigh's hand. "That's why I had to make sure I chose the perfect ring before I asked you to be my wife."

Calleigh's hands started shaking uncontrollably when she saw Deion open the Tiffany box and take out a stunning 7 ct. diamond cluster halo ring with accent diamonds around the band.

"I already think of you as my wife. I just wanna make it official. Will you marry me?" Calleigh couldn't even respond because the tears wouldn't stop flowing. "It's okay, baby. You don't have to cry," Deion said, caressing the side of her face.

"You really do love me," she said, as if surprised.

"Of course I love you. You my everything. So will you marry me?"

"Yes! Yes! Yes! I'll marry you." Deion slipped the massive sparkler on Calleigh's finger while Alex and Anya clapped for them.

"I never thought in my life I would see my best friend Deion proposing to a woman. I'm so happy for you, man," Alex said, walking over and giving him a hug. "Congratulations to you also. Welcome to the family," Alex added, hugging Calleigh too.

"Girl, I can't believe you're getting married," Dominique

said, inspecting Calleigh's engagement ring. "And this fuckin' ring is everything. I'm so jealous, but in a good way." Dominique giggled. "I mean Deion spoils you rotten. You are one lucky bitch."

"Yeah, I am aren't I? Sometimes I forget..." Calleigh's voice trailed off.

"Forget what?"

"Nothing."

"So when you gonna start planning the wedding?"

"Deion is handling it. He already chose the wedding planner. Of course he wants an over-the-top spectacle."

"I wonder what Passion said when she heard the news."

Calleigh frowned at Dominique. "I'm tempted to toss this pillow at your head. Who fuckin' cares what Passion thinks."

"Don't get mad at me, girl. I'm just throwing it out there. I know she somewhere salty though. Trust me, like every other chick in Atlanta, she never thought Deion would put a ring on nobody except for maybe Alex."

"Girl, you is stupid!" The women both laughed.

"Deion is very protective when it comes to Alex, probably to a fault. But enough about Alex and Passion because it's all about me and Deion."

"You right. You won, girl. Marrying Deion is like landing one of the kings of New York. Him and Alex are even bigger than what Laron and his Get Money Crew was. Since Deion is the king, I guess that makes you the queen." Dominique winked.

"Come on, let's go before we're late for our spa appointment."

"Man, let me get outta here. I'm already late to Demonte's birthday party," Deion said, getting up from the bar.

"Have you told Passion yet about the engagement?" Reggie asked.

"Nope. But I think the streets have already informed her."

"Probably so 'cause they definitely been buzzin' about you gettin' married."

"If she doesn't bring it up, I am gonna mention it. Even if the streets have already informed her I still want her to hear from me."

"Well, enjoy the party, but be careful. Female problems are the worst sort of problems. You see what almost happened to Alex." Reggie smirked, joking, but dead ass serious.

"When it comes to Passion, I got that under control. She knows her place and gives me no problems. Now let me get outta here."

When Deion arrived to Passion's house the birthday party was in full swing. There were kids everywhere, most running around in the backyard. Half the adults were drinking and the other half were making sure the kids didn't tear up the house.

"Uncle Deion," Demonte came running up screaming when he saw Deion enter the kitchen. "I'm so happy you're here," he said, hugging him.

"I wouldn't miss your birthday party for the world. Where's your mother?"

"Passing out the cake to all my friends. Thank you for all the presents. You the best uncle ever." Demonte smiled, holding on to Deion's leg.

Deion picked Demonte up and let him sit on his shoulders, carrying him outside to the backyard. He watched from a short distance as Passion played the perfect hostess, making sure all the guests had everything they needed.

In that moment, Deion understood his connection to Passion. He wanted to be her savior because he could never save his own mother. When Deion was a little boy, he dreamed of his mother meeting some rich man who would get her off drugs, be a father to him, and get them out of the projects. He waited for that dream to come true for so long, but once his mother overdosed he knew it would never come true. Now, in Deion's mind he was making that dream come true through Passion. He had gotten her out of the strip club. She was able to be a wonderful mother to her son, and he was like the father to Demonte that he never had. It had come full circle and it finally made sense to Deion.

"Where have you been?" Calleigh questioned, turning on the light next to the bed.

"Hey baby, I thought you were sleep?"

"No, I've been waiting for you to get home."

"You didn't have to wait up for me. Go back to sleep. I'ma take a shower."

"You haven't answered my question. Where have you been?"

"Reggie had some business to handle for me so I had to cover for him at the lounge."

"So you've been at the lounge all night."

"Yeah, that's what I said, isn't it."

"You fuckin' liar! Unless you have a twin, how were you able to be at the lounge and at Passion's house for her son's birthday? Explain that shit to me."

"Who told you I was there?'

"Why does that matter?"

"Because whoever told you, I'ma fuck them up 'cause they need to mind they own motherfuckin' business."

"Why the fuck were you at that party! I'm your fiancé. You supposed to be home with me, but you at her house with her son, like you all are one big happy family!"

"Yo shut up and stop being so fuckin' dramatic. Who wearin' my fuckin' ring? Who living in this fuckin' mansion wit' me? Who fuckin' got a closet full of clothes and jewelry that it look like a department store? Ya dumbass worry about the wrong shit."

"Did you fuck her tonight? Is that why you so late? I know a kid's birthday party doesn't last until three o'clock in the morning."

"Calleigh, stop fuckin' crying!"

"Answer the question!"

"What if I did, it don't matter. She has nothin' to do wit' us. I promised you she would never bother you again. Has she bothered you? Hell no! 'Cause she know her position. And you need to know your position... you my wife. You belong to me. But don't ever question me about some woman again unless one steps to you. But that ain't gon' neva happen so we good. Now go to sleep."

All Calleigh could do was lay down and cry herself to sleep.

Chapter 21

TELL THE TRUTH AND SHAME THE DEVIL

"Man, what you doing here?" Deion asked when he opened the door and saw Alex.

"Calleigh called and said you wanted me to meet you here."

"She did?" Deion questioned with a raised eyebrow. "That's strange. She's in the restroom. I'll ask her about it when she comes out."

"So you didn't tell her you wanted me to meet you here?"

"Nope. You know the lounge ain't even open today. We just stopped by on our way to brunch so I could pick something up."

"That is odd."

"She's been acting odd for the last few weeks anyway."

"Is there trouble in paradise already? You haven't even gotten married yet."

"We had a slight situation a few weeks ago."

"What type of situation?"

"Some runnin' off at the mouth motherfucker told her I was at Passion's house for Demonte's birthday party."

"Please don't tell me you still fuckin' Passion on the low. Didn't you learn anything from my Isabella and Joaquin love triangle?"

"Man, chill. We'll talk about this later. Here she come," Deion said, shushing Alex up.

"Alex, I'm glad you got here so quickly," Calleigh said, walking up on them.

"Alex said you told him I said to meet me here."

"Yes, I did."

"Why? I didn't tell you to do that."

"Because I thought it was time for the three of us to have a heart to heart."

"A heart to heart? Calleigh, what the fuck?"

Deion stared at her confused.

"You heard me. Tell him, Deion. Tell Alex, your so-called best friend, what you did to him."

"Yo, what the fuck is wrong wit' you. Go get in the fuckin' car and shut the hell up!" Deion barked, not understanding what had gotten into Calleigh, but ready to smack the shit outta her.

"I'm not getting in the car. I'm standing right here until you tell Alex what you did."

"Is someone gonna tell me what the hell is going on?" Alex asked, completely baffled.

"Is you high, drunk, or just actin' fuckin' stupid? Or are you still pissed about Passion so you tryna 'cause unnecessary problems?" Deion barked.

"Good ol' Passion. That's your real bottom bitch, right. If only you could've cut her out of our lives then maybe I wouldn't have to do this. But it's too late now. I've already pressed go."

"I'm 'bout to get you the hell outta here before I fuck you up for being a shit starter," Deion spit, reaching forward to grab her arm.

"Don't you fuckin' touch me!" she screamed, before quickly reaching in her purse and pulling out a 9mm.

"Yo, what the fuck!" Alex and Deion belted simultaneously. They were both furious because neither of them were carrying a weapon. Deion did remember there was a gun hidden in a secret compartment at the bar but that was on the other side of the room, which made it useless at this point.

"Give me that gun, Calleigh," Deion demanded, not knowing if he was dealing with a snapped situation or what.

"Both of you move over there and sit down," Calleigh said, pointing towards a booth.

"Are you serious wit' this shit!" Deion was becoming amped. His anger had reached a boiling point. "You my motherfuckin' fiancé. Bitch, you wearin' the rock I put on yo' finger and you got a gun pointed at me and my man. On the real you betta calm the fuck down, 'cause you takin' it to a place ain't no coming back from," Deion warned.

"Sit down, both of you," Calleigh said, not backing down. "I don't wanna have to use this gun, but I will be heard, so sit down."

Alex and Deion glanced at each other and

nodded their heads, then did as she said. "Calleigh, we sittin' down. Whatever you got to say, can you just get it out? There's no need for this to get ugly," Alex said, trying to be the voice of reason.

"You're right and since Deion isn't in the mood for a confession, I'll do it for him. This story is gonna take a little while so the two of you should get comfortable."

"Yo', I promise you, I'ma fuck you up when you done wit' this little show you puttin' on. Embarrassing me and embarrassing yo' motherfuckin' self."

"You are so full of yourself, Deion." Calleigh giggled. Although she was laughing there was nothing but disdain in her eyes. "You ruined my life."

"What is you talkin' about. Bitch, I gave yo' ass everything. I ain't neva treated a woman as good as I treated you. I put a ring on yo' finger. I was 'bout to make you my wife," Deion roared, rising up, banging his fist on the table. "I give you the world and you done gon' off on the deep end."

"Sit down!" Calleigh yelled, pointing her gun directly at Deion's head. "You can have this ring and shove it up yo' ass!" Calleigh continued yelling, taking the ring off her finger and tossing it at Deion. "Why would I marry a man like you who lies and cheats! The only man I should've ever married was Laron."

"Laron." Deion mumbled his name. "Who the fuck is Laron and what I got to do wit' him."

"Are you talkin' about Laron, the leader of GMC?" Alex asked, immediately recognizing the name since he was the one he blamed for Dahlia's death.

"Yes, that's exactly who I'm talking about."

"Laron was yo' man." Deion stated as his jaw began flinching. "So you fucked wit' me on some revenge type shit?"

"Yes, because you killed him... all of them, and for what."

"Calleigh, your man and his crew were responsible for the rape and murder of my fiancé. They had to die," Alex said matter of factly.

"See that's where you're wrong, Alex. You were made to believe that to keep you from finding out the truth, isn't that right, Deion?"

Alex cut his eyes at Deion waiting to hear his

response. "Yo, I can't believe I ever trusted you. I shared everything wit' you. You sick bitch." Deion swallowed hard, two seconds away from snapping her neck.

"The only sick person in here is you. You raped and killed your best friend's woman, left a bag of GMC drugs to make Alex believe they were responsible so you all could kill them, and take over their drug territories. Deion, you thought you committed the perfect crime and you almost got away with it."

"Deion, tell me she's lying. That this is all a figment of a hurt woman's imagination. Tell me this is all a lie," Alex said, as his once calm demeanor was being taking over by a cloud of darkness.

"Of course she's lying! This miserable bitch just mad that we killed her man and now she tryna cause beef between us," Deion stated adamantly.

"Lies! Lies! Lies! Nothing but lies! You thought your secret died with Tommy and his girlfriend. But before you killed Tania she had already told me the truth. That's who called you, Alex and said she knew who really killed your fiancé. But Deion had to shut her up so he murdered Tania just like he murdered

Dahlia."

"Man, she's lying. You can't believe nothing that comes out of her mouth."

"Alex, if you stop and think you'll be able to put the pieces together and realize that everything I'm saying is true. You killed an innocent man and his crew based on a lie."

"She's fuckin' lyin', Alex. Are you satisfied now, Calleigh? You did all this just to try and turn me and Alex against each other. That's some weak shit."

"I'm glad you think so because telling Alex the truth about what you did was just the icing on the cake. Right now the feds are raiding all of your warehouses, stash houses, and arresting the members of your crew. The two of you will be going to jail for a very long time, unless of course, Alex kills you first."

"You trife whore! You a dead bitch!" Deion roared, lunging towards Calleigh. She pulled the trigger, releasing a warning shot.

"Next time, I won't miss. The bullet will go straight in your heart. Now get back over there," Calleigh said, keeping her gun aimed at the men while walking towards the front entrance. "Good riddance, Deion. I pray this is the very last time I'll ever have to see your face again, you evil sonofabitch."

The moment Deion heard the door shut he jumped up to go after Calleigh. "Where do you think you're going?" Alex asked, pulling Deion's arm, stopping him in his tracks. "We're not leaving here, until you tell me the truth and I mean the whole truth."

Chapter 22
DEAD END

"Laron would be proud," Clip said, kissing Calleigh on the cheek. "I knew you would be perfect to bring Deion down."

"You always said that and was so adamant about it. But how were you so sure?"

"Don't take this the wrong way, Calleigh because I don't mean it in a negative way."

"Say it."

"Laron molded you to be the perfect kingpin's woman. The way he dressed you, had you style your hair, how you conduct yourself overall. Deion is a kingpin, once he saw you I knew his ego wouldn't allow him to let you get away. You would have to be his and no one else's."

"Wow, I never knew that was the reason."

"Yeah, when I said you were the only woman that could pull this off, it's because I knew it would take a lot more than a pretty face and a nice body to make a man like Deion fall in love."

"Good thing you were right, Clip."

"Yes indeed, because you were my last hope."

"You should have seen the repulsion on Deion's face when I told him the truth. He literally wanted to kill me," Calleigh said, trying not to break down in front of Clip. "If I hadn't had my gun, I would be dead right now."

"That wouldn't have even been a concern if you'd listened to me."

"I had to confront Deion so he would know it was me that brought him down. While he rots in jail, I'll be the face that haunts him. Unless he never makes it to jail because Alex kills him first."

"That's no longer our concern. It's over for Alex and Deion. I don't care if them niggas rot in jail or kill each other. Because of you, we were able to get retribution for Laron and GMC."

"I can't take all the credit. You were the mastermind, Clip. If it weren't for you I would still be in New York, feeling like shit, mourning over Laron. Truth be told, when you asked me to come here and help you, during the entire plane ride I kept debating with myself."

"Why?"

"Because I didn't think I could pull it off. But I learned a lot from Laron. He was a great boyfriend and excellent teacher. He schooled me on so much including the power of persuasion. Although none of this brings him back, I can now move on because I got justice for him and GMC."

"When you say move on, does that mean you leaving?"

"Yes, I'm going back to New York to finish grad school like Laron would've wanted."

"Before you go I have something for you."

"What is it?"

"Stay here."

While Calleigh waited, she walked over to the window that had a view of the private lake. It was beautiful outside. You could hear the birds chirping, the trees blowing, and peacefulness ensuing. The tranquility was soothing to her soul, something that hadn't been within her reach for months. Calleigh could never admit this to Clip and she could barely admit it to herself but during her charade she had developed real feelings for Deion and she hated herself for it. She even wondered if it wasn't for his relationship with Passion would she had ever gone through with turning on him. Calleigh had psyched herself into believing that pretending to be in love with Deion was more difficult than actually having to deal with Laron's death. The difficult part was that she wasn't pretending, she was in love with him.

Waking up with Deion in the morning, having to feel him inside of her, and saying the words I love you felt like a knife going through her heart in the beginning. But soon that pain turned into pleasure and her body yearned to have him inside of her at all times. But Calleigh had made a promise to Clip and even if she wanted to, she knew Clip would never let her live happily ever after with the man that killed his best friend. She also did love Laron so she tried to bury her feelings for Deion. She became more determined to gain Deion's trust so she could get all the evidence she needed to hand him over to the feds. Calleigh knew she had to get Deion out of her life for good because the more she spent time with him the deeper she fell in love.

"Calleigh," Clip called out for the second time, but she was so engrossed in reliving her time with Deion that she didn't even hear him. "Calleigh," Clip said again, this time touching her shoulder.

"Oh, you startled me," she said jumping.

"Whatever you were thinking about had you somewhere else. I called out to you a few times before I touched you."

"Yeah, my mind was someplace else but I need to be getting out of here. I have to make a quick stop at the townhouse and get my dog, Diamond, before I hit the road."

"This is what I wanted to give you before you left," Clip said, handing Calleigh a metal briefcase.

"What's inside?"

"Open it."

Calleigh sat the briefcase on the table and opened it. "Clip, I can't take this. There has to be at least a million dollars in here," Calleigh said, looking at the stacks of 100-dollar bills.

"It's actually two million."

"I didn't help you bring down Deion and Alex for money. I did it for Laron."

"I know. But he would want you to have this money, Calleigh. Laron took very good care of you while he was alive and he would want me to do the same in his death. So please, take it."

"Thank you for looking out for me like this."

"If you need me, don't ever hesitate to call."

"I won't." Calleigh smiled, giving Clip a kiss on the cheek before leaving.

"Alex, I can't believe you standin' here questioning me over something that psycho bitch said. That bitch just mad 'cause we killed her man. I can't believe I wasted all that time and money on that dumb ho," Deion spit, ready to punch his fist through the wall.

"So none of what Calleigh said is true. You had nothing to do wit' Dahlia's death."

"Didn't I just say no! Why are you makin' me waste my time explaining a lie away. I need to go find her snake ass so I can kill her before she get the fuck outta town, 'cause I know that's what she's about to do."

"How did she know about that phone call I received about Dahlia's death? How did she know about the bag of GMC drugs left by Dahlia's body?"

"Maybe she was the one that made the phone call. Have you ever thought about that? She been orchestrating this bullshit for I don't know how fuckin' long. Laron was her man so maybe he told her that they left the bag of drugs there. Again, I don't fuckin' know but it don't have nothing to do wit' me. But I do know one thing, you worryin' 'bout the wrong thing. She turned us over to the fuckin' feds. We got much bigger shit to be thinking 'bout."

"I've known you all my life, Deion. You like my brother. I love you. I also know you just about as well as I know myself. So I know when you lyin'," Alex said, as his lips quivered. For a moment his body had become paralyzed with the realization as the tragic truth gradually seeped in. "How could you do this to me? To us?" was the only question Alex could get out as his eyes began to bleed with pain.

"Man, what are you talkin' about?" Deion asked, throwing his hands up in frustration. "I told you that Calleigh was lyin'! Why you lettin' her do this to us?"

"Stop lying to me!" Alex roared. His voice was so loud it sounded like the glass was about to shatter. We were everything to each other. You were all I had," Alex howled, balling his hands into fists, clutching them to his chest. You've ruined everything!"

"No, that bitch Dahlia ruined everything! Before she came into the picture we was a team. We had plans," Deion stated, hurling his finger at Alex. Then you fell in love wit' her in what, two motherfuckin' days. You wanted to throw away everything we worked so fuckin' hard to build... for her... her! A broad you knew nothin' about. You were willing to walk away from your best friend... your brother." Deion paused, trying to blink away the emotions that were about to blur his vision but one tear managed to escape. "You chose her over me. We made a pact that we would never let anybody come between us. You left me no choice. Dahlia had to go."

"The lure of the game has destroyed you. I don't even know who you are anymore."

"I'm the same motherfucker that gave you power. I kept my end of the bargain. It was you that tried to renege on the game."

"Fuck you!" Alex bawled, racing towards Deion and striking him with a sharp left hook. Alex switched over to throw a right jab at his jaw but Deion blocked the punch. Alex caught him with an uppercut to the chin, but when he swung again, Deion sidestepped releasing a flurry of his own punches upon Alex, a powerful one connected with Alex's ribs causing him to hunch over. Deion struck again, this time a right hook that landed on Alex's nose, which sent blood gushing out. As Alex tried to stop the bleeding, Deion used the opportunity to go retrieve the gun from the hidden compartment at the bar.

Determined to finish their fight, Alex ran towards Deion, but was met with looking down the barrel of a gun. "I don't want to kill you, Alex, so get the fuck out my way," Deion cautioned.

Alex stood, blocking Deion's path. "You gon' have to kill me 'cause if I have my way you ain't leaving here alive," Alex threatened, panting heavily. Deion gripped the gun tightly as if about to squeeze the trigger, but instead without warning, he pounced it against the side of Alex's head, knocking him out.

When Calleigh pulled up to her townhouse, even though she planned on being in there for no more than a few minutes she took her briefcase with her. With two million dollars at risk she was taking no chances of it coming up missing. She held onto it tightly as she unlocked her front door. Calleigh heard Diamond barking as she ran towards her. "Hey there, cutie pie," she said bending down to pick her up. Diamond started licking Calleigh all over her face, excited to see her. "It's time for us to get ready to go."

"You ain't goin' nowhere," she heard Deion say as he pressed the gun against the back of her head. "Get the fuck in the house," he said, pushing her forward, then slamming the door shut and locking it.

"Deion, don't do this."

"I know you ain't askin' me to have mercy on you? You used me, destroyed my friendship wit' Alex, and turned me in to the feds. If I'm going to jail they might as well add a murder charge to it."

"You truly have no soul."

"I didn't think I did either until I fell in love wit' you. I gave you everything including my heart. But it was all a game to you... wasn't it?"

"No, it wasn't a game, but you murdered Laron and his entire crew for no reason. Innocent people died because of your lies."

"Ain't nobody in this game innocent. We can all die at any time because we choose to spend our days and nights sinning. So don't stand there and try to make me feel like I'm a monster. 'Cause if I'm a monster then so is every other hustler that roams these streets."

"I took something away from you and you took something away from me. Can we just call it even and let me start my life over away from here?"

"That's what you call yourself doing? Taking the dog I gave you, driving off in the car I bought you, and what's in the briefcase?" Deion questioned, yanking it away from Calleigh and opening it up. "So this is what turning on me got you. A briefcase full of money."

"I didn't turn on you for the money. You can have it. This was never about money for me. I did hate you at first, but I fell in love with you. I'm still in love with you. I didn't want to admit it but it's true. But the damage is done and I know it's too late for us. So I just want to go back to New York and start my life over," Calleigh pleaded.

"You right, the damage is done. It's too late for us. But you still belong to me and I told you, I would never let you go. You shoulda thought twice before you decided to come into my life, enter my world, and play these games. Because once you did that, you made me the judge, jury, and executioner. And although I'll always love you, I sentence you to death," Deion stated, unloading the entire magazine on Calleigh, riddling her body with bullets. She lay dead in a puddle of blood holding her Maltese. Deion grabbed the money and left.

A day, a week, and then a month passed and no one had seen or heard from Deion and Alex. They both seemed to have vanished without a trace until one Friday afternoon, without notice, Alex showed up at his attorney's office.

"I believe there is a warrant out for my arrest," Alex announced the moment he walked through George Lofton's door.

"Do you know if it's federal or state?"

"I believe it's federal."

"How do you know? Have they come to your home?"

"I haven't gone home since I got word they were raiding some warehouses and other spots that could possibly have drugs, and guns, things of that nature."

"If they have raided your home too, would they have found anything illegal there?"

"No. I don't keep anything there. But I'm

positive they've been to my home."

"Why?"

"Because they've already frozen all of my bank accounts."

"I see. I'll make some calls. Are you prepared to turn yourself in?"

"Yes, that's why I'm here. I've used the last few weeks to get some things in order. Now I'm ready to fight whatever charges the feds bring my way."

"Well, you've already financially compensated me so you don't have to worry about your legal fees, which was smart of you to do, given that your bank accounts have been frozen."

"I'm assuming your business partner will be facing the same charges as you?"

"I would think."

"Although I won't be able to represent him, you also gave me more than enough for his defense. He'll be able to afford the best lawyer money can buy. I can refer some excellent attorneys."

"That won't be necessary. You can return Deion's money to me. He'll be securing his own attorney."

"Say no more. I will return that money to you immediately and I'll get started on your case. I'm sure the feds will want you to surrender, but I'll try to get bail set though I'm sure they'll be against it. I have to ask, if they're offering a plea deal will you be willing to accept it?"

"I'm no snitch and I won't agree to testify against anybody. If a plea deal requires me to do that, then I'll fight the charges and take my chances in a court of law."

"Understood. I'll be in touch as soon as I get all the pertinent information. Is your number still the same?"

"No, I tossed that phone. I have a new number."

"Okay, well leave it with my secretary. I'll speak to you later on."

After Alex left his attorney's office, he headed to the five star hotel he'd been staying at for the last few weeks. He wanted to reach out to Anya but he wasn't sure if the feds were monitoring her phone calls and following her movements. Alex decided it would be best to call once he knew when he would turn himself in.

Besides Anya, there were only two other people that had held Alex's mind hostage since being in hiding—Dahlia and Deion. Alex had replayed the night Calleigh revealed the truth about Dahlia's death too many times to count. His nights were literally haunted by the revelation and his days were restless. He tried to figure out had there been any signs he missed and one thing kept flashing through his mind. The night Deion shot and killed Tommy when he was trying to tell Alex something. Back then Deion had excused his abrupt actions because he feared Tommy was about to shoot him, but now Alex knew the truth. Deion feared Tommy would divulge that the real culprit in his fiancé's rape and murder wasn't GMC, but his own best friend.

The more that Alex had to accept this as truth, the more enraged he became. He contemplated tracking Deion down and unleashing the same fate he gave Dahlia. The only reason he wasn't dead was because Alex had no idea where Deion was.

Deion was laying back, relaxing in one of the private, white draped cabanas poolside at the W South Beach. On each side of him was a stripper that he had met at the King of Diamonds strip club the other night. The women sipped on top shelf frozen margaritas while eating grilled blackened mahi sandwiches. For the last couple of days their job description only consisted of fucking and sucking Deion at his convenience. They were well aware that their services would no longer be required at any given moment, as they would be replaced with new chicks. So the ladies simply enjoyed the good food, free drinks, and the money Deion hit them off with for as long as it lasted.

Since escaping Atlanta, Deion had found refuge in Miami staying at the W South Beach. After murdering Calleigh, he took the two million dollars she had, plus he retrieved money he kept stashed at one of his secret locations. Deion didn't even bother going home and getting additional money he kept there because he figured the feds were already there waiting to arrest him. Like Alex, all of Deion's bank accounts had been frozen but he had more than enough to keep him living good until he could figure out what to do next. Deion also had one other spot where he stashed some money, but decided not to take it with him. When and if the authorities caught up to him, Deion wanted to make sure he had additional paper set aside for attorney fees.

That moment would come much sooner than he had anticipated. When the feds entered his private cabana, Deion had his eyes closed, enjoying the fellatio one of the strippers was giving him, oblivious to it all.

"Deion Owens, we have a warrant for your arrest..." After Deion heard those words he opened his eyes and saw that he was surrounded by federal agents who had guns drawn. After that, Deion blocked out everything they said next. He knew the gig was up and just pulled up his swim trunks before putting his hands behind his back.

"Ain't this some shit," he mumbled when the handcuffs gripped his wrists. Deion knew at that moment his life would never be the same again.

Chapter 23
I Gave You The Power

One Year Later...

The sun beamed on Alex's face as a gentle hot breeze swept past him. His gaze locked onto the cloudless sky for a second as he walked towards the Federal Correctional Institution Edgefield located in South Carolina, approximately 25 miles north of Augusta, Georgia. It was a medium security prison that housed roughly 1,700 inmates, one of them being Deion.

"I didn't think you would come," Deion said, as he sat across from Alex.

"At first I wasn't," he admitted.

"What changed your mind?"

"The birth of my son."

"You a father... congratulations." Deion smiled. "I'm happy for you, man. I see you wearing a wedding band, too."

"Yeah, Anya and I got married."

"You finally got that family you always wanted. You deserve it. Your son is lucky, you gon' be a great father."

"Our sons were supposed to grow up together... like us. Except not in the projects like we did, not knowing where our next meal would come from. Remember we made a pact when we were coming up that our kids would have everything we never did."

"I remember. Back then I didn't even think we would live long enough to grow up and have kids of our own. I would just co-sign on all that talkin' you did 'cause we was young as shit but you sounded mad confident. You believed it would happen for us. I guess you was partially right."

Alex put his head down for a second before

continuing. "I hate you so much." He put his head down again. "But man, I love you, too. That's why this shit hurt. We coulda had it all. I still don't understand how everything got so fucked up. I've spent the last year trying to figure it out."

"I'm not built like you, Alex. You gotta heart. I'm just a foul fuck."

"Bullshit. If it wasn't for you takin' all those charges I'd be sittin' in a jail cell right next to yours. That's the shit that pisses me off about you. You do so much fucked up diabolical shit that makes me believe you beyond redemption, but then you turn around and let me go free while you rot in jail."

"That's how it's supposed to be. You earned it... you deserve the power not me."

"I guess I'm supposed to owe you and feel guilty right?"

"Guilty for what? I raped and killed your fiancé," Deion stated, leaning forward in a low but firm tone. "You didn't turn me in for that. The least I can do is take these drug charges and do this bid solo. You don't owe me nothin' and damn sure not no guilt."

"It wasn't supposed to end like this."

"You right, Alex, it wasn't. I messed up. I've fucked up before but somehow I was always able to clean the mess away, but not this time. Believe it or not, knowing you married, with a son and you have a family makes it easier for me to sit down and do this bid."

"Our visitation time is about to be up," Alex said, looking down at his watch.

"I know. Can you do me a favor before you go?"

"What is it?"

"Can I see a pic of your son?" Alex nodded his head yes before pulling out a picture from his wallet. "Handsome kid. He gon' be a heartbreaker." Deion grinned.

"Yeah, just like the man he was named after... you."

"You named your son after me?" Deion asked, swallowing hard to keep his eyes from watering up.

"Yes, I did. I didn't plan to. But after he was born and I held him in my arms for the first time, it just felt right. If I had been locked up, he would've never been conceived. He was able to come into this world because you let me be free and for that reason alone I forgive you."

"I don't deserve your forgiveness but thank you." The two men stood and hugged each other before Deion watched his best friend walk away but not out of his life. Deion knew Alex would be back to visit at least once a month, until he finished doing his 20-year prison sentence.

The End

Bad Bitches Only

ASSASSINS...

EPISODE 1
(Be Careful With Me)

JOY DEJA KING

Chapter One

HE LOVES ME

Bailey strutted out the Hartsfield-Jackson Atlanta International Airport, in her strappy, four inch snakeskin shoes, wearing matte black wire frame square sunglas ses and a designer suit tailored to fit her size six frame perfectly. The brown beauty looked like she was a partner at a powerful law firm, when actually she was barely a second year law student. But school was the least of her worries. Bailey had other things on her mind, like the promise ring she was wearing. It cost more than some people's home. Don't get it confused, this wasn't a promise of sexual abstinence. This was a promise of marriage, from her boyfriend of five years, Dino Jacobs.

"Keera," I was just about to call you girl," Bailey said, getting in her car.

"I was shocked as shit when you answered. I was expecting to leave a voicemail. You said you was gonna be in some conferences all day," Keera replied.

"Girl, I was but I checked out early. I'm back in the A."

"You back in Atlanta?!" Keera questioned, sounding surprised.

"Yep. That's why I was calling you. So we could do drinks later on tonight at that spot we like." Baily was getting hyped, as she was dropping the top on her Lunar Blue Metallic E 400 Benz.

"Most definitely...so where you headed now."

"Where you think...home to my man! Stop playin'," Bailey laughed, getting on interstate 75.

"I know yo' boo, will be happy to see you."

"Yep and his ass gon' be surprised too. He thinks I'm coming back tomorrow night. But I missed my baby. Plus that conference was boring as hell. All them snobby ass lawyers was workin' my nerves."

"Get used to it, cause you about to be one," Keera reminded her.

"Yeah but only cause Dino insisted. You know

I wanted to attend beauty school. I love all things hair and makeup. I have zero interest in law. But that nigga the one paying for it, so it's whatever," Bailey smacked.

"Girl, don't be wasting that man money. You better get yo' law degree and handle them cases!" Keera giggled.

"Okaaaay!! I believe Dino just want me to be able to represent his ass, in case anything go down," Bailey snickered.

"Well, let me get off the phone so you can get home."

"Keera, I know how to talk and drive at the same damn time," she popped.

"I didn't say you didn't but umm I have a nail appointment. You know they be swamped on a Friday," Keera explained.

"True. Okay, go get yo' raggedy nails done," Bailey joked. "Call me later, so we can decide what time we meeting for drinks."

"Will do! Talk to you later on."

When Bailey got off the phone with Keera, she immediately started blasting some Cardi B. The music, mixed with the nice summer breeze blowing through her hair, had her feeling sexy. She began imagining the dick down she'd get from Dino, soon as she got home.

"Here I come baby," Bailey smiled, pulling in the driveway. She was practically skipping inside the house and up the stairs, giddy like a silly schoolgirl. You'd think hearing Silk's old school Freak Me, echoing down the hallway, in the middle of the afternoon, would've sent the alarm ringing in Bailey's head. Instead, it made her try to reach her man faster.

It wasn't until she got a few steps from the slightly ajar bedroom door, did her heart start racing. Next came the rapid breathing and finally came dread. You know the type of dread, that seems like it's worse than death but you don't know for sure because you've never actually died. It was all too much for Bailey. Her eyes were bleeding blood. She wanted to erase everything she just witnessed and rewind time.

I shoulda kept my ass in DC, she screamed to herself, heading back downstairs and leaving the house. Once outside, Bailey started to vomit in the bushes, until there was nothing left in her stomach.

ORDER FORM

Name:

Address:

City/State:

Zip:

QUANTITY	TITLES	PRICE	TOTAL
	Bitch	$15.00	
	Bitch Reloaded	$15.00	
	The Bitch Is Back	$15.00	
	Queen Bitch	$15.00	
	Last Bitch Standing	$15.00	
	Superstar	$15.00	
	Ride Wit' Me	$12.00	
	Ride Wit' Me Part 2	$15.00	
	Stackin' Paper	$15.00	
	Trife Life To Lavish	$15.00	
	Trife Life To Lavish II	$15.00	
	Stackin' Paper II	$15.00	
	Rich or Famous	$15.00	
	Rich or Famous Part 2	$15.00	
	Rich or Famous Part 3	$15.00	
	Bitch A New Beginning	$15.00	
	Mafia Princess Part 1	$15.00	
	Mafia Princess Part 2	$15.00	
	Mafia Princess Part 3	$15.00	
	Mafia Princess Part 4	$15.00	
	Mafia Princess Part 5	$15.00	
	Boss Bitch	$15.00	
	Baller Bitches Vol. 1	$15.00	
	Baller Bitches Vol. 2	$15.00	
	Baller Bitches Vol. 3	$15.00	
	Bad Bitch	$15.00	
	Still The Baddest Bitch	$15.00	
	Power	$15.00	
	Power Part 2	$15.00	
	Drake	$15.00	
	Drake Part 2	$15.00	
	Female Hustler	$15.00	
	Female Hustler Part 2	$15.00	
	Female Hustler Part 3	$15.00	
	Female Hustler Part 4	$15.00	
	Female Hustler Part 5	$15.00	
	Female Hustler Part 6	$15.00	
	Princess Fever "Birthday Bash"	$6.00	
	Nico Carter The Men Of The Bitch Series	$15.00	
	Bitch The Beginning Of The End	$15.00	
	Supreme...Men Of The Bitch Series	$15.00	
	Bitch The Final Chapter	$15.00	
	Stackin' Paper III	$15.00	
	Men Of The Bitch Series And The Women Who Love Them	$15.00	
	Coke Like The 80s	$15.00	
	Baller Bitches The Reunion Vol. 4	$15.00	
	Stackin' Paper IV	$15.00	
	The Legacy	$15.00	
	Lovin' Thy Enemy	$15.00	
	Stackin' Paper V	$15.00	
	The Legacy Part 2	$15.00	
	Assassins	$11.00	

Shipping/Handling (Via Priority Mail) $7.50 1-2 Books, $15.00 3-4 Books add $1.95 for ea. Additional book.
Total: $_____FORMS OF ACCEPTED PAYMENTS: Certified or government issued checks and money Orders, all mail in orders take 5-7 Business days to be delivered

CPSIA information can be obtained
at www.ICGtesting.com
Printed in the USA
LVHW030039130821
695154LV00005B/735

9 781942 217305